THE MAN WITH
THE GOLDEN ARM

THE MAN WITH THE GOLDEN ARM

Based on a novel by
Nelson Algren

Screenplay by
**Walter Newman
and
Lewis Meltzer**

A film by
Otto Preminger

Published 2025 by Maple Spring Publishing

Front cover design by David Rheinhardt of Pyrographx
Interior design by Jason Snyder

Library of Congress Cataloging-in-Publication Data is available upon request

ISBN: 979-8-3505-0178-0

10 9 8 7 6 5 4 3 2 1

THE MAN WITH THE GOLDEN ARM

Cast

Frank Sinatra *as* Frankie "Dealer" Machine

Eleanor Parker *as* Sophia "Zosh" Machine

Kim Novak *as* Molly Novotny

Arnold Stang *as* Sparrow

Darren McGavin *as* "Nifty Louie" Fomorowski

Robert Strauss *as* Zero Schwiefka

John Conte *as* Drunkie John

Doro Merande *as* Vi

George E. Stone *as* Sam Markette

George Mathews *as* Williams

Leonid Kinskey *as* Dominowski

Emile Meyer *as* Captain Bednar

Shorty Rogers *as* himself (bandleader at audition)

Ralph Peña *as* himself (bassist at audition)

Shelly Manne *as* himself (drummer at audition)

We see a busy Chicago street in the 1950s. A bus pulls up to a stop. Frankie "Dealer" Machine gets out, carrying a suitcase and a drum in a case, played by Frank Sinatra. He goes down the street. The neighborhood is seedy. He passes a strip club. He then passes in front of a building. Two attractive women, undoubtedly prostitutes, are looking out the windows. One of them says:

PROSTITUTE

Hi, Frankie.

FRANKIE "DEALER" MACHINE

Hello.

Frankie walks on, past a pool hall. He looks inside. Then past a policeman, who is hauling a suspect out of a pawnshop into a police car.

POLICEMAN

Get in there.

Frankie passes a sign on a window: BEER. He looks inside and sees several men taunting a paraplegic, who is missing one arm and one leg. Nifty Louie Fomorowski, a sharply dressed but shifty-looking man with a small mustache, is holding a glass of whiskey to the man's nose.

"NIFTY LOUIE" FOMOROWSKI

Nothing like that first drink of the day. Come on, drink up, enjoy it. Hey, they tell me you're some dancer.

The paraplegic man shakes his head.

"NIFTY LOUIE" FOMOROWSKI

Well, how about a little dance anyway?

The paraplegic shakes his head.

"NIFTY LOUIE" FOMOROWSKI

No?

Nifty Louie makes as if to pour the glass of whiskey on the floor. The paraplegic hops around pathetically, to the men's laughter. We see Frankie, looking inside the window. He seems a bit saddened by the prank, but then he has an affectionate smile: these men are his friends.

Frankie goes into the bar, where Sparrow is in a booth, combing a schnauzer. Sparrow is a young man, unshaven, with black-rimmed glasses and a baseball cap. He is of the type that used to be called a punk. Frankie pulls off his glasses.

SPARROW

Hey, give me back . . . Don't horse around . . . What's a big idea?

Sparrow looks up and recognizes Frankie, who puts the glasses back on Sparrow.

SPARROW

Frankie? Frankie! Frankie, when did you get back?

Sparrow hugs Frankie.

SPARROW

How are you? You all right? You know . . .

FRANKIE "DEALER" MACHINE

The monkey's gone.

SPARROW

Let me look at you. Let me look at you. Not even a posty card.

FRANKIE "DEALER" MACHINE

You can't read anyway.

SPARROW

Well, you could have drawn pictures.

FRANKIE "DEALER" MACHINE

There you go, punk. How's the lost dog business?

SPARROW

Yeah. As soon as they see me hanging around, people start locking up their mutts. I tell you folks just don't have that trust in their fellow man anymore. You know what I mean?

Laughter behind Frankie and Sparrow as the barflies continue to taunt the paraplegic, who is still hopping around.

SPARROW

Hey, Yantek, look who's out!

Yantek, the middle-aged bar proprietor, comes over and shakes Frankie's hand enthusiastically.

YANTEK

Frankie, you are all right? Clean?

FRANKIE "DEALER" MACHINE

Yep.

YANTEK

Good kid.

FRANKIE "DEALER" MACHINE

Enough already. Buy me a drink.

YANTEK

Sure.

Frankie goes over to the bar, where he greets a number of barflies, all of whom know him well. One of them is Vangie, a middle-aged woman. Nifty Louie is also there.

MALE SPEAKER

Look what the cat dragged in.

VANGIE

Frankie, honey.

MALE BARFLY 1

You was gone so long, I thought maybe you was made warden.

MALE BARFLY 2

Hey, you're looking good, Dealer.

FRANKIE "DEALER" MACHINE

Put on six pounds.

BARFLY 3

Wow! Six pounds.

BARFLY 1

He's gone so long I thought maybe he was made warden.

VANGIE

How was it down there? Frankie?

FRANKIE "DEALER" MACHINE

Greatest place you ever see, Vangie.

BARFLY 2

He means Lexington.

FRANKIE "DEALER" MACHINE

I'm telling you, ball games, great food. I even learned how to play the drums.

BARFLY 2

You make it sound as if I missed something by not going to jail years ago. It's a prison, no?

FRANKIE "DEALER" MACHINE

More of a hospital kind. Let me show you something.

BARFLY 3

Ah, federal pens is always best, ask anybody.

VANGIE

Well, I know . . .

BARFLY 1

He's gone so long, I think he's made warden.

Frankie produces a large drum out of his case.

FRANKIE "DEALER" MACHINE

Have you seen anything so pretty?

Sparrow raps on the drum.

FRANKIE "DEALER" MACHINE

Don't touch.

SPARROW

Hey, how'd you sneak them out, Frankie?

FRANKIE "DEALER" MACHINE

The guys give me them up there in the band.

BARFLY 2

They let you have a band?

FRANKIE "DEALER" MACHINE

Yeah, I was in it. They chipped in and bought me these
when I left.

SPARROW

Wow.

Nifty Louie is standing by the doorway.

"NIFTY LOUIE" FOMOROWSKI

Long time, dealer. How was it there? Bad?

FRANKIE "DEALER" MACHINE

It was all right.

"NIFTY LOUIE" FOMOROWSKI

Six months. You can hardly wait, I bet. Come over to my place.

FRANKIE "DEALER" MACHINE

No thanks, Louie.

"NIFTY LOUIE" FOMOROWSKI

You broke? Now ain't you being stupid? It's for free.

FRANKIE "DEALER" MACHINE

I don't need it is all. I kicked it.

"NIFTY LOUIE" FOMOROWSKI

Oh, kicked it. One of them.

FRANKIE "DEALER" MACHINE

I mean it.

"NIFTY LOUIE" FOMOROWSKI

Sure. I'll be around.

Frankie goes and sits down to Sparrow, who has gone back to combing the schnauzer.

SPARROW

Frankie, don't do it. Don't start up with that peddler again.

FRANKIE "DEALER" MACHINE

Me, I'd rather chop my arm off before I let him touch it. This Dr. Lennox who took care of me down at the hospital, he was a good guy. He told me at least 10 times. He said, "Frankie, when you get out of here, you take even one fix, you're hooked again." Don't worry about me, buddy boy, let's get out of here.

Sparrow goes over to the bar and hands over the schnauzer to Yantek.

SPARROW

Yantek, take care of this asset for me. I got a customer coming to get it.

YANTEK

Okay, Sparrow.

Frankie and Sparrow leave. We see Nifty Louie looking off thoughtfully, smiling cagily.

Frankie and Sparrow are now outside on the street, walking.

SPARROW

Don't let him give you no gas.

FRANKIE "DEALER" MACHINE

Him? I'm not going to be around here long enough to let him bother me. I'm going to get me a job in a big-name band.

SPARROW

You're kidding.

FRANKIE "DEALER" MACHINE

What do you think I'm strengthening my wrist for, Buddy-o? The guy who teaches me drumming down there says that I'm a natural. Can't miss, he says; arms made of pure gold.

SPARROW

You mean a job winding these drums?

FRANKIE "DEALER" MACHINE

I got everything planned too. Going to call myself Jack Duvall.

SPARROW

Probably I ain't going to see you around so much then, huh?

FRANKIE "DEALER" MACHINE

Yeah, maybe I can set something up for you. Carrying around instruments or something.

SPARROW

Wow!

They reach the stoop of Frankie's apartment building and climb up the stairs.

FRANKIE "DEALER" MACHINE

Traveling around the country, high-type nightclubs. How's that sound to you, punk?

SPARROW

When is it going to be? When?

FRANKIE "DEALER" MACHINE

Right away, today. I'm the kind of guy, boy, when I move, watch my smoke. But I'm going to need some good clothes though.

SPARROW

Oh, well you go on up, I'm going to find you something.

FRANKIE "DEALER" MACHINE

Yeah. Size 39.

SPARROW

39.

FRANKIE "DEALER" MACHINE

Stripes.

SPARROW

Stripes.

FRANKIE "DEALER" MACHINE

Something nice.

Sparrow goes off. Frankie goes into the apartment building and up the stairs. From a second-floor apartment comes a loud clangor.

PROPRIETOR

(off-camera)

You stop that noise, you and your husband, or I throw you both out. You hear?

VI

(off-camera)

I'll make all the noise I want.

PROPRIETOR

Who is landlord? Me. You do like I say.

Frankie comes up the stairs to see the proprietor, a middle-aged man with an Eastern European accent, and Vi, a scrawny middle-aged woman.

VI

(to Proprietor)

Your mother's eye socks, I do like you say.

Vi sees Frankie.

VI

Frankie Machine. Oh, you look great. How you feeling, Frankie? I mean . . .?

FRANKIE "DEALER" MACHINE

Fine, Vi. Just fine. Hi, landlord.

PROPRIETOR

She and husband fight all the time, holler, throw things.

FRANKIE "DEALER" MACHINE

Nothing changes.

PROPRIETOR

This is a respectable house, and I am respectable man.

VI

Respectable, my eye. Come on, get out, you're late for
the parole board.

Frankie takes his gear up to the third floor. He sets it down
hesitantly on the landing, then picks it up again and goes to
the door of an apartment. He opens the door and goes in. His
wife, Zosh, a beautiful young blonde woman in a nightgown, is
sitting in a wheelchair. There is a crudely written sign, "Welcome home Frankie" hanging on the wall.

SOPHIA "ZOSH" MACHINE

Oh. Frankie, you're home!

Frankie and Zosh embrace.

SOPHIA "ZOSH" MACHINE

Oh, Frankie, I love you so much! Oh! I missed you so.

She clutches him and kisses him eagerly.

SOPHIA "ZOSH" MACHINE

I've been so lonely, Frankie, without you. I'm so lonely.

FRANKIE "DEALER" MACHINE

Zosh, stop crying. Zosh, let me look at you.

SOPHIA "ZOSH" MACHINE

My eyes are going to be all red.

FRANKIE "DEALER" MACHINE

Naw, you look fine, Zosh.

SOPHIA "ZOSH" MACHINE

You promise? Is the cold sore gone?

FRANKIE "DEALER" MACHINE

Yeah, you look real good.

Frankie takes off his hat and closes the apartment door.

SOPHIA "ZOSH" MACHINE

I had this cold, and I wanted to look real nice for you when you came back and I was afraid it wouldn't be gone. So I put this goofy salve on to dry it. Oh, Frankie.

FRANKIE "DEALER" MACHINE

Oh Zosh, everything's going to be all right.

SOPHIA "ZOSH" MACHINE

Oh, you didn't see.

She points to a cake sitting on a side table below the sign.

SOPHIA "ZOSH" MACHINE

Look, Vi got the cake by the bakery, but the sign I made, it's sort of like for a welcome home.

FRANKIE "DEALER" MACHINE

Geez. It's like a real party or something.

Frankie picks up the cake and tastes the frosting.

FRANKIE "DEALER" MACHINE

It's real nice, Zosh.

SOPHIA "ZOSH" MACHINE

How are you, Frankie?

FRANKIE "DEALER" MACHINE

I'm clean.

SOPHIA "ZOSH" MACHINE

You sure?

FRANKIE "DEALER" MACHINE

I kicked it for keeps.

SOPHIA "ZOSH" MACHINE

Did it hurt? How was it there for you?

FRANKIE "DEALER" MACHINE

Oh, they treated me fine down there. There was this doctor, this Dr. Lennox, he was really good to me.

Frankie moves his drum case across the room. Zosh wheels her wheelchair back toward him.

SOPHIA "ZOSH" MACHINE

Frankie, Frankie, did you miss me?

FRANKIE "DEALER" MACHINE

Of course, I missed you, Zosh. What kind of silly question is that? Of course I missed you. Honest, no kidding.

He moves his suitcase over.

SOPHIA "ZOSH" MACHINE

What do you have there?

FRANKIE "DEALER" MACHINE

You'll see. Oh, I brought you something.

He takes out a metallic necklace made out of tinfoil and hands it to her.

SOPHIA "ZOSH" MACHINE

Oh, it's an exquisite thing.

FRANKIE "DEALER" MACHINE

You like it? I made it myself out of cigarette wrappers.

SOPHIA "ZOSH" MACHINE

It's just an exquisite thing is all. You made it?

FRANKIE "DEALER" MACHINE

Yeah. For a hobby like. See, part of the cure is to keep yourself busy doing things you enjoy. Like for instance, I wanted to learn the drum and music and Dr. Lennox got them to help me do it. During the day, I was kept busy enough, but sometimes at night, I'd get restless. I wanted to keep my mind off the craving, I made that.

SOPHIA "ZOSH" MACHINE

There's something important I got to tell you.

FRANKIE "DEALER" MACHINE

What?

SOPHIA "ZOSH" MACHINE

Well, I forget right now.

Zosh produces a whistle, which is hanging on her neck, and blows it.

FRANKIE "DEALER" MACHINE

A whistle?

SOPHIA "ZOSH" MACHINE

Oh, I was scared sometimes being alone. So Vi got it for me. I should blow for her when I wanted her. Go on, you were telling me.

Frankie takes out his drums and starts setting them up.

FRANKIE "DEALER" MACHINE

Oh, well, the first thing you do when you get there, you talk to a doctor for about two hours.

SOPHIA "ZOSH" MACHINE

Oh, I know. I know what it is. I know what I had to tell you. Vi took me to this movie. And the girl's kid brother had a friend in it. Now who do you think he looked like?

FRANKIE "DEALER" MACHINE

Who?

SOPHIA "ZOSH" MACHINE

You! That was a good movie. The stage show was really good too. We owe Vi 80 cents for the movie. I was broke, and we owe her for the cake too.

FRANKIE "DEALER" MACHINE

How come you didn't have any money? Schwiefka didn't kick in regular?

SOPHIA "ZOSH" MACHINE

No.

FRANKIE "DEALER" MACHINE

He was supposed to! It was his joint they raided, not mine. I was just the dealer. I kept my mouth shut and took the rap. If he didn't send 50 a month regular, how much did he?

SOPHIA "ZOSH" MACHINE

Well, he sent 50, but not regular. You see, Vi had to kick in for me sometimes.

FRANKIE "DEALER" MACHINE

She took good care of you? You have fun with her?

Frankie turns on the radio. Swing music is playing.

SOPHIA "ZOSH" MACHINE

Yeah, but not like when you're here. It was terrible being alone, Frankie, and my legs, when they hurt, she don't massage like you.

FRANKIE "DEALER" MACHINE

What do they say by the clinic, Zosh?

SOPHIA "ZOSH" MACHINE

I stopped going by that goofy clinic.

FRANKIE "DEALER" MACHINE

The clinic must know what's right, Zosh. You gotta start the clinic again; you gotta get well.

SOPHIA "ZOSH" MACHINE

I dreamed that this new doctor around the corner, he cured me. I'd have gone to him already, but he ain't free like the clinic. But now you're back making money again by Schwiefka, I'll go.

FRANKIE "DEALER" MACHINE

I'm finished with Schwiefka; I don't deal for him no more.

SOPHIA "ZOSH" MACHINE

But you always deal. You're a dealer. You're the best dealer in the business.

FRANKIE "DEALER" MACHINE

No more. I'm a drummer now.

SOPHIA "ZOSH" MACHINE

Don't make jokes, Frankie. I never know when you're making jokes.

FRANKIE "DEALER" MACHINE

Who's joking, Zosh? Listen.

Frankie starts playing his drums, accompanying the music on the radio.

FRANKIE "DEALER" MACHINE

Nice, huh? This Dr. Lennox, I told him my whole life story from what I was born almost, and about you and me. But he told me that if I lived when I got out like I lived before I went in there, chances are I would be hooked again in no time. So that's why I want to get with a band.

Frankie drums.

FRANKIE "DEALER" MACHINE

Listen, how's that?

SOPHIA "ZOSH" MACHINE

Cute. What did you tell him about me, this doctor?

FRANKIE "DEALER" MACHINE

I told him about getting some money and getting you
well, and he said getting with a band was a good way
to go at it. He even gave me the name of a guy in town
right here to get a job.

SOPHIA "ZOSH" MACHINE

That's nice. I mean, if this man with a job ever heard
of this great doctor. Most times these things just don't
come through.

FRANKIE "DEALER" MACHINE

I got this.

Frankie pulls a letter out of his jacket.

SOPHIA "ZOSH" MACHINE

What is it?

FRANKIE "DEALER" MACHINE

It's a letter from Doc. I think I'll go call him now.

SOPHIA "ZOSH" MACHINE

Now? Let's talk about it tomorrow.

FRANKIE "DEALER" MACHINE

I'll be right up, Zosh.

SOPHIA "ZOSH" MACHINE

You haven't even tasted the cake.

FRANKIE "DEALER" MACHINE

It'll only be a minute! I'll be right up.

SOPHIA "ZOSH" MACHINE

No, now, Frankie. First, just a piece of nice—cake.

She lights a candle on the cake, but Frankie is out the door before she finishes.

Down on the first floor, Frankie goes to the pay phone and makes a call while Drunkie John, a disreputable-looking man in a sport coat and tie, is standing at the front door, waiting for Molly, who is off camera.

DRUNKIE JOHN

Hey, you coming, baby?

MOLLY NOVOTNY

(*off camera*)

Yeah, Yeah, I'm coming, John.

DRUNKIE JOHN

Hey, Molly?

MOLLY NOVOTNY

(*off camera*)

Yeah. Good.

Frankie is talking on the phone.

FRANKIE "DEALER" MACHINE

I want to talk to Mr. Harry Lane, please.

DRUNKIE JOHN

(to Molly)

How about it? Huh?

FRANKIE "DEALER" MACHINE

Machine. Frankie Machine. Yeah, I got a letter of intro-
duction for him, from Dr. Lennox.

Molly Novotny, a beautiful blonde, comes out of the apartment.
She talks to Frankie while he is still on the phone.

MOLLY NOVOTNY

Hello, Frankie.

FRANKIE "DEALER" MACHINE

Dr. Martin Lennox.

   (turning to Molly, putting his hand on the receiver)

How you been, Molly?

Molly comes up very close to Frankie.

MOLLY NOVOTNY

All right.

DRUNKIE JOHN

Come on, baby, let's go.

MOLLY NOVOTNY

(to Frankie)

A guy I met when you were away.

Frankie is talking into the phone.

FRANKIE "DEALER" MACHINE

Mr. Lane, I got a letter for you.

DRUNKIE JOHN

(to Molly)

Come on. Yeah, come on. What do you say, kid?

Drunkie John and Molly go out.

FRANKIE

(into the phone

This afternoon? Huh? Would you? I sure do appreciate it, Mr. Lane. Thank you so much. Okay, bye-bye.

Sparrow runs into the hallway carrying a new suit under his coat. He rushes up the stairs but halts when he sees Frankie on the phone. He shows Frankie the suit.

SPARROW

Frankie! A new thing by Brax department store! No salesgirls. Just help yourself. It's what they call a honor system. What's the matter, Frankie?

Sparrow shows him the suit.

SPARROW

Feel that material, and I figured as long as I'm there . . .

Sparrow pulls a new shirt out from under his own shirt. Frankie looks pensive.

SPARROW

Nice, huh? Are you all right? Frankie?

FRANKIE "DEALER" MACHINE

I got the drumming job.

SPARROW

Already! Wow!

FRANKIE "DEALER" MACHINE

When I move, I move like a streak, punk.

Back in the apartment, Frankie is putting on the suit while Zosh is brushing her hair.

FRANKIE

Think it looks all right, Zosh?

SOPHIA "ZOSH" MACHINE

How come you ask me all of a sudden?

FRANKIE "DEALER" MACHINE

I just want to know if it looks all right, Zosh.

SOPHIA "ZOSH" MACHINE

And my name ain't Zosh, it's Sophia.

FRANKIE "DEALER" MACHINE

What's the matter?

SOPHIA "ZOSH" MACHINE

Nothing's the matter, except how would you feel if your spine was hurting?

FRANKIE "DEALER" MACHINE

Why didn't you say so?

SOPHIA "ZOSH" MACHINE

On account of your first day back, I just didn't want you should worry.

FRANKIE "DEALER" MACHINE

Don't be like that, Zosh. Is it bad?

He starts massaging her back. Sparrow, who has been there below, helping Frankie into his suit, pops up and helps Frankie into his jacket.

SOPHIA "ZOSH" MACHINE

Well, maybe the new doctor will do me some good. Huh?

FRANKIE "DEALER" MACHINE

We'll go see him when I get back.

SOPHIA "ZOSH" MACHINE

Oh, take me now, Frankie!

FRANKIE "DEALER" MACHINE

Zosh, I got this appointment. You know how much it means to me. Huh? We'll go as soon as I get back.

SOPHIA "ZOSH" MACHINE

Please, Frankie.

FRANKIE "DEALER" MACHINE

I'll hurry.

SOPHIA "ZOSH" MACHINE

Frankie, well, give me a little more massage then, first, huh?

FRANKIE "DEALER" MACHINE

Zosh, I'm doing this for you to get some money so you can get a good doctor.

SOPHIA "ZOSH" MACHINE

Oh, please, Frankie?

FRANKIE "DEALER" MACHINE

Look, I'll get you a dog too. How's that? Huh?

(to Sparrow)

Get her a dog, will you?

SPARROW

I'll give the matter my personal attention. Just have confidence in the management.

FRANKIE "DEALER" MACHINE

Wish me luck, Zosh.

Frankie kisses her. He and Sparrow leave the apartment.

SOPHIA "ZOSH" MACHINE

Oh, Frankie. Wait, wait, Frankie.

She opens the door and starts to blow her whistle feebly, but she stops. Then she locks the front door, gets up from the wheelchair, and goes to the window to look out at him.

Out on the street. Frankie is nattily dressed in his new suit and a bow tie. He walks down the street with Sparrow.

FRANKIE "DEALER" MACHINE

I can't be in two places at once. What could I do?

SPARROW

Yeah. She just don't realize . . .

FRANKIE "DEALER" MACHINE

Oh, shut up, punk. You just don't realize. How would you like to be nailed to a chair?

They pass by the bar. Zero Schwiefka, a tough-looking man smoking a cigar (as he always is), looks out the bar window at him. He raps on the window, beckoning Frankie in. Frankie and Sparrow go into the bar.

ZERO SCHWIEFKA

Frankie, Frankie, how are you? Well, it didn't do you no harm, did it, Frankie? Oh, you look good.

FRANKIE "DEALER" MACHINE

That's right, Schwiefka, it was a real country club.

Schwiefka, Frankie, and Sparrow go over to the bar. Yantek pours him a whiskey. Frankie sees Molly and Drunken John at a table nearby in the background. The bartender pours drinks for Frankie and Schwiefka. Schwiefka fingers Frankie's suit.

ZERO SCHWIEFKA

Hmm? They give you this when they let you out?

SPARROW

Give him, nothing! I borrow by Brax.

ZERO SCHWIEFKA

You know, I came as soon as I heard you were out. I figured, he's worried about getting his job again. Tell him don't worry, Schwiefka don't forget so quick. Job's waiting.

FRANKIE "DEALER" MACHINE

You need a dealer, you say?

ZERO SCHWIEFKA

Me? No. I've been dealing myself and, man, I built up a game like nobody's business. I have a great following. The play is bigger than ever.

FRANKIE "DEALER" MACHINE

I hear you wasn't doing so good

ZERO SCHWIEFKA

From who? When I say great, I don't mean a lot—a few, but loaded.

FRANKIE "DEALER" MACHINE

So what do you want me for?

ZERO SCHWIEFKA

Like I'm telling you, I take care of my friends.

SPARROW

Can I polish your halo, Schwiefka? Only a quarter.

ZERO SCHWIEFKA

Knock it off, punk. Look, I've been doing all right, but I don't say that the customers like me better than they like you. The dealer makes the house. I know that. What do you say?

FRANKIE "DEALER" MACHINE

No.

ZERO SCHWIEFKA

You're dealing for some other joint?

FRANKIE "DEALER" MACHINE

I ain't dealing for nobody. I ain't dealing for nobody no more.

ZERO SCHWIEFKA

Is that the way you repay me? Didn't I send money to Zosh? I've gone and tell all my friends that you'll be working for me again. What am I supposed to do?

FRANKIE "DEALER" MACHINE

As far as I'm concerned, you can go back to matching pennies with school kids.

Schwiefka gives Frankie a dirty look, throws a dollar on the bar, and leaves.

Drunkie John calls the bartender from his table.

DRUNKIE JOHN

Hey, Yantek? Yantek?

FRANKIE "DEALER" MACHINE

(to Sparrow)

Who is he?

SPARROW

Drunkie? His name's Johnny something. He's house-
man for Gobercheck's poolroom.

Frankie gestures toward Drunkie John and Molly.

FRANKIE "DEALER" MACHINE

Is that a thing with him?

SPARROW

They see each other. You want to meet him?

FRANKIE "DEALER" MACHINE

No. So long, Yantek.

YANTEK

See you, Frankie.

Frankie and Sparrow go out into the street. A police car pulls
up in front of them immediately. Two policemen, one of them
Officer Parker, beefy and middle-aged, get out.

OFFICER PARKER

Hey, you. Get in, dealer.

FRANKIE "DEALER" MACHINE

Who? Me? What for?

Sparrow tries to go off, but the other policeman grabs him.

OFFICER PARKER

You too, punk.

FRANKIE "DEALER" MACHINE

I didn't do nothing. Oh, wait a minute, Parker. Listen, I'm on my way to get a job. It's important to me. You can pick me up some other time. I just need an hour. Be a good guy, will you?

OFFICER PARKER

Shut up.

The policemen push Frankie and Sparrow into the car.

The scene changes to police captain Bednar's office, like the other officers tough and middle-aged but wearing street clothes. He is seated at his desk, shaving himself with an electric razor.

Officer Parker brings in Frankie and Sparrow.

SPARROW

What are you walking talking for? Are you looking to get sued for libel or something? I could sue you right now.

CAPTAIN BEDNAR

You're looking good, dealer, really good. When they let you out?

FRANKIE "DEALER" MACHINE

Monday they let me out. What's the charge, Parker?

POLICEMAN

Shoplifting from Brax the suit.

SPARROW

Who told you a thing like that?

POLICEMAN

A little bird.

FRANKIE "DEALER" MACHINE

A little bird with a cigar.

SPARROW

Schwiefka.

CAPTAIN BEDNAR

I thought you could stay out of trouble. Two days. Dealer, dealer.

FRANKIE "DEALER" MACHINE

Listen, Bednar, I got a chance for a job playing with a band. Honest. If you don't believe me, call the guy on the phone. He'll tell you. Well, just give me a half hour, please.

OFFICER PARKER

Sure, you can wear my badge too.

CAPTAIN BEDNAR

Book him and hold his suit.

FRANKIE "DEALER" MACHINE

A guy needs a half hour. Give me a break, will you?

CAPTAIN BEDNAR

I don't make the rules, dealer.

Frankie and Sparrow are being led downstairs into a jail cell by Officer Parker, who is handling Sparrow roughly.

SPARROW

Now, I tell you, you can't hold me, I'm incapable. I ain't smart enough to be running around, but I'm too goofy to be locked up.

The policeman has Sparrow by the neck.

SPARROW

The neck, will you let go the neck? I got a complaint. Let go the neck.

Frankie and Sparrow are led into a cell. There are two junkies there.

JUNKIE 1

(To Officer Parker)

Hey you. I'm talking to you. Oh, the old silent treatment, huh? All right, let's have your number, fella. I'll show you, you can't give me the business. Your goose is cooked, copper.

Frankie sits down, next to a second junkie, who yawns with a tormented look on his face. Frankie moves away. Sparrow sits next to him.

SPARROW

Frankie, you got a cigarette? Do a cigarette trick? You know, just to break the dirty monotony.

Frankie puts the cigarette through his fingers. Then he opens his hand. The cigarette is missing. Frankie opens both his hands. They are both empty. Then he pulls the cigarette out from behind Sparrow's ear.

SPARROW

Wow!

Schwiefka appears in front of the jail cell.

ZERO SCHWIEFKA

Dealer.

Frankie and Sparrow go up to the bars.

ZERO SCHWIEFKA

Hello, dealer. I come running as soon as I heard. You want I should get you out, dealer?

FRANKIE "DEALER" MACHINE

You fink.

ZERO SCHWIEFKA

The store will drop the charges, but 37 bucks is a lot of dough. How do I know you'd pay me back?

FRANKIE "DEALER" MACHINE

You fink.

ZERO SCHWIEFKA

It'd be different if you was dealing for me. If you want to deal for me, I can get you out.

Frankie grabs Schwiefka by the lapels through the bars of the cell.

FRANKIE "DEALER" MACHINE

Dirty, lousy stool pigeon.

ZERO SCHWIEFKA

I don't know what you mean. Just trying to do you a favor. Yes or no?

FRANKIE "DEALER" MACHINE

Okay.

Scwiefka strides off.

SPARROW

He took off like a whipped dog. He's scared of you, Frankie.

FRANKIE "DEALER" MACHINE

Nobody's ever been scared of me.

SPARROW

Them Krauts was scared of you. You was a big man in the army.

FRANKIE "DEALER" MACHINE

Big man. I was the guy picked the fly spots out of the black pepper.

Junkie 2 flings himself in a panic against the bars.

JUNKIE 2

Get me out! I can't take it! Get me out!

Two guards go into the cell. Junkie 2 falls on the floor in panic.

JUNKIE 2

I want a fix! I want a fix! A fix! Give me a fix. Can you gimme a fix? I want a fix!

The two guards haul off Junkie 2. We see Frankie pressing his face against the bars in despair, his eyes in tears as we hear the howls of Junkie 2 in the distance.

We are now in Schwiefka's poker room. Frankie is dealing.

FRANKIE "DEALER" MACHINE

Check what? Let say a buck. Big aces, and here we go, down and dirty.

We see Sparrow escorting a losing gambler out.

SPARROW

Better luck next time, friend.

Sparrow opens the door for him and locks it again when the man is out. Sparrow goes over to where a game is going on, with several men around a table, Frankie dealing. Barfly 1 and Nifty Louie are among the players. Schwiefka is supervising.

FRANKIE "DEALER" MACHINE

Check what? Man with a hammer bumps a buck. Jack calls. Bucket of paint all red.

SCHWIEFKA

Coffee.

Sparrow goes to get some coffee.

FRANKIE "DEALER" MACHINE

Doesn't mean a thing if you haven't got the king. Winner every hand. You bet more, you get more. Slip a hand, make me laugh.

"NIFTY LOUIE" FOMOROWSKI

You still take tips, dealer, or don't they pay so good in the music game? What happened to that big job you had lined up? You stink up the joint? Give us a fresh deck.

FRANKIE "DEALER" MACHINE

I decide when we need a fresh deck at this table.

SPARROW

Hey, Louie, borrow me a dirty dollar?

"NIFTY LOUIE" FOMOROWSKI

Get back to the door, lamebrain.

SPARROW

I take orders only from Frankie.

"NIFTY LOUIE" FOMOROWSKI

Don't give me your lip, you cheap little hustler.

SPARROW

Hustler, smushler. I'm legit compared to some. Ain't no 14-year-old junkies waiting around to see me.

Nifty Louie jumps up and grabs Sparrow by the lapels.

"NIFTY LOUIE" FOMOROWSKI

You want to die?

Frankie continues the game.

FRANKIE "DEALER" MACHINE

And here we go, down and dirty.

Nifty Louie lets go of Sparrow and sits back down at the game.

At the table, Frankie, dealing, slips up and deals one card up.

"NIFTY LOUIE" FOMOROWSKI

Hey.

FRANKIE "DEALER" MACHINE

I'll deal the next one down. Sorry.

"NIFTY LOUIE" FOMOROWSKI

What's it a sign of when a dealer's hands begin to shake?

FRANKIE "DEALER" MACHINE

Schwiefka, could you take the slot for a while, will you?

Frankie gets up from the table. Schwiefka sits down in his place.

ZERO SCHWIEFKA

All right, man, new deal. Okay, men, here we go, down and dirty. Ace, 7.

Frankie leaves. We see him going down the stairs outside. He stops and lights a cigarette nervously. Nifty Louie comes out and follows him down the stairs.

"NIFTY LOUIE" FOMOROWSKI

You know what's eating at you? You shot off your mouth about kicking it for keeps. So now you're ashamed of even thinking—well what you're thinking, ain't that right? You know I don't talk about my customers. So who'll be the wiser? Why fight it, dealer? For who? For what? Come over my place. What do you say?

Frankie goes off. "Nifty Louie" Fomorowski whistles behind him.

"NIFTY LOUIE" FOMOROWSKI

I'll be around.

Frankie goes down the street to a nightclub called Club Safari. He goes in. There is a floor show going on, with strippers and a band. Frankie goes over to the bar and sees Molly, who is at a stand, clerking for a gambling game.

FRANKIE "DEALER" MACHINE

They told me you were working here and I was passing by and I thought I'd come in and have a drink.

MOLLY NOVOTNY

Well, I've been here a while.

FRANKIE "DEALER" MACHINE

Doing any good?

MOLLY NOVOTNY

All right. Small cut of the game, usual cut of the drinks.

A waiter comes up to the two of them.

BARTENDER

I ain't got all night, Jack.

FRANKIE "DEALER" MACHINE

Right, have something.

MOLLY NOVOTNY

Rye.

FRANKIE "DEALER" MACHINE

Two doubles.

The waiter goes off.

MOLLY NOVOTNY

You didn't have to do that, Frankie.

FRANKIE "DEALER" MACHINE

No reason you should go losing money by wasting your time talking to me.

MOLLY NOVOTNY

You know you're no waste. I've been hoping you'd come see me.

FRANKIE "DEALER" MACHINE

You know how it is, Molly.

MOLLY NOVOTNY

Sure. So busy now.

The waiter brings over two large drinks. Frankie gives him a dollar.

FRANKIE "DEALER" MACHINE

Here's to it Molly-O.

MOLLY NOVOTNY

Molly-O. I ain't heard that since you went away. You're looking good, Frankie.

FRANKIE "DEALER" MACHINE

Feel good.

MOLLY NOVOTNY

They tell me you're going to be a drummer now.

FRANKIE "DEALER" MACHINE

Yeah, I got an appointment with a man tomorrow.

MOLLY NOVOTNY

Oh, that's swell.

FRANKIE "DEALER" MACHINE

Yeah. Probably I won't get the job though.

MOLLY NOVOTNY

Sure, you will.

FRANKIE "DEALER" MACHINE

Probably I don't play good enough.

MOLLY NOVOTNY

I bet you play fine. You was always whistling and drumming on tables and things, real good too.

FRANKIE "DEALER" MACHINE

Ah.

MOLLY NOVOTNY

I mean it. You got a natural rhythm.

FRANKIE "DEALER" MACHINE

I was thinking maybe I'd take a stage name. Jack
Duvall.

MOLLY NOVOTNY

Jack Duvall. Yeah, that's real class.

FRANKIE "DEALER" MACHINE

It is, ain't it?

MOLLY NOVOTNY

That's a swell name; just fits you, Frankie.

FRANKIE "DEALER" MACHINE

This guy I'm going to see tomorrow, he books all the
big bands. If I get in with him, boy, I wear a tux.

MOLLY NOVOTNY

You'd look swell in a tux.

FRANKIE "DEALER" MACHINE

I already got the drums.

Drunkie John comes up to them.

DRUNKIE JOHN

I need a buck; ante up, kid, huh?

Molly opens her purse and gives him a dollar. Drunkie John
goes away furtively.

MOLLY NOVOTNY

I got lonely. I needed somebody. And he's a poor beat guy who needs somebody too.

FRANKIE "DEALER" MACHINE

Everybody needs somebody, but you can do better than him.

MOLLY NOVOTNY

Can I, Frankie?

FRANKIE "DEALER" MACHINE

Molly, I thought a lot about you while I was away, about you and me and Zosh. It would never work out between you and me as long as she was upstairs sitting in that chair. It'd be different if she didn't love me and she wasn't so helpless. You can't make a fool of somebody who loves you and they're so helpless. That's why I didn't come around sooner. And that's why I ain't coming around no more. You understand?

MOLLY NOVOTNY

Sure. Sure, I understand.

Frankie strokes Molly's bare shoulder.

FRANKIE "DEALER" MACHINE

You're a good girl, Molly.

MOLLY NOVOTNY

Sure. Real good.

Frankie makes to leave.

MOLLY NOVOTNY

Frankie, good luck with that fella tomorrow.

We now see the front of an enormous building: the Lane Building. Then we see Frankie in Mr. Lane's large, well-appointed office. Mr. Lane, a man in late middle age in a double-breasted suit and smoking a cigar, looks at a letter.

MR. LANE

You are not the first to come to me with a letter from Dr. Lennox. I've taken care of a lot of you people.

FRANKIE "DEALER" MACHINE

The doc, he told me.

MR. LANE

I like doing it, understand. So don't feel that this is charity or anything like that. Now, have you played professionally before?

FRANKIE "DEALER" MACHINE

Only down at Lexington.

MR. LANE

I see. Well, then, you wouldn't mind auditioning. I mean I know some bandleaders who might have an opening, but they'd have to be sure that you could play.

FRANKIE "DEALER" MACHINE

Oh sure, sure.

MR. LANE

All right then. There's only one thing, Frankie. You see, a good many people like yourself—well, they mean well, but they're, well, they're weak. They let me down. I mean, I go to all this trouble, vouch for them; they go back on the habit. It makes me look bad.

FRANKIE "DEALER" MACHINE

Well, I wouldn't, honest.

MR. LANE

All right. I'm telling you this because, well, once a man lets me down, I'm done with him. He comes back on his knees, and don't think that some of them haven't.

FRANKIE "DEALER" MACHINE

I wouldn't let you down, Mr. Lane.

MR. LANE

Good. I'll call you, let me see, a week from Friday, about noon. All right?

Mr. Lane hands the letter back to Frankie.

FRANKIE "DEALER" MACHINE

Fine. I sure do appreciate it.

MR. LANE

Oh, forget it.

FRANKIE "DEALER" MACHINE

Bye.

MR. LANE

Goodbye.

Back in the apartment, Frankie is massaging Zosh's leg while she brushes her hair and looks in a mirror.

SOPHIA "ZOSH" MACHINE

You like my hair better this way or up swept, Frankie? Huh? Well, you can at least tell me. It ain't my fault he don't phone. What did I say? Just don't hold your breath until you hear from that guy. That's what I said. He told you noon. It's almost six o'clock already. So how could you still think he'll phone? Honest, I'm surprised that you . . .

Frankie gets up and goes sulkily to the other end of the room.

SOPHIA "ZOSH" MACHINE

I just don't want you to eat your heart out is all. Forget the whole thing, Frankie. I bet he has. You think he got nothing better to do than worry about you? You think he don't sleep nights on account of Frankie Machine? Bet he don't get no rest . . .

The phone rings downstairs. Frankie rushes out to get it. Zosh follows him in her wheelchair, looking over the railing.

Frankie, going downstairs, passes Dr. Dominowski, a foreign-looking quack, going up

DR. DOMINOWSKI

Excuse me.

Frankie answers the phone downstairs.

FRANKIE "DEALER" MACHINE

Hello?

The proprietor comes up behind him.

FRANKIE "DEALER" MACHINE

Oh, just a minute. For you.

PROPRIETOR

(picking up the phone)

Hello?

Dr. Dominowski comes up to the second floor and sees Zosh still in the hallway.

SOPHIA "ZOSH" MACHINE

Are you Dr. Dominowski?

DR. DOMINOWSKI

Yes. I came as soon as I could.

They go in the apartment, Frankie following.

DR. DOMINOWSKI

Well, how are you feeling, little lady?

SOPHIA "ZOSH" MACHINE

See, the doc asks, how am I feeling?

DR. DOMINOWSKI

Ah, I'll have you feeling fine in 1, 2, 3.

The doctor has a large electronic device.

FRANKIE "DEALER" MACHINE

What is this?

DR. DOMINOWSKI

It happens, friend, to be an electric blood reverser and spine manipulator. It helps to reverse the blood.

FRANKIE "DEALER" MACHINE

What's the gimmick?

DR. DOMINOWSKI

Gimmick? It happens so, brother, that I am a member of the American Association of Medical Hydrology, Psychology, and Divine Healing. Where is the socket?

Dr. Dominowski hands him a plug. Frankie plugs in the machine. The doctor feels Zosh's hand.

DR. DOMINOWSKI

Cold hands, poor circulation. Eat lots of hot things. Chili peppers, hot sauces.

SOPHIA "ZOSH" MACHINE

Pickles.

DR. DOMINOWSKI

No more than three a day. Now lean forward and we'll vibrate the vertebraes.

He applies a hand-held electrical device to Zosh's spine.

SOPHIA "ZOSH" MACHINE

You know how I got like how I am? My spine was hurt.

DR. DOMINOWSKI

Oh, I can see that. The ligaments and the vertebrae is locked together.

SOPHIA "ZOSH" MACHINE

In a car accident, I was hurt, three years ago, May 11th. Maybe you read about it in the papers, huh?

Zosh pulls out a scrapbook and shows him a picture. Frankie starts pacing around the room. Dr. Dominowski's machine buzzes.

SOPHIA "ZOSH" MACHINE

This is the car it happened in. That's me laying there. My husband was the one driving the car, and he was drunk.

DR. DOMINOWSKI

Drunk, eh?

The doctor looks at Frankie accusingly.

SOPHIA "ZOSH" MACHINE

He got me in this accident and smashed me up good, so that I can't walk no more, or dance no more, nothing. And he married me right here, in the hospital chapel.

FRANKIE "DEALER" MACHINE

Zosh!

Frankie takes his coat and dashes out of the apartment.

DR. DOMINOWSKI

Feeling a little better?

Zosh strokes the scrapbook affectionately. Dr. Dominowski continues to apply his device to her back.

SOPHIA "ZOSH" MACHINE

Uh-huh. Much better.

Frankie goes into Yantek's bar next door, where Sparrow has a dog sitting on a table near the entrance. Nifty Louie is sitting at the bar. He sees Frankie in the mirror.

SPARROW

Help yourself. Hey Frankie, guess what? I got that dog for Zosh. Free spirit! Every claw and hair of him is a champion.

Sparrow pours some beer into a glass for the dog.

FRANKIE "DEALER" MACHINE

Champion or what?

SPARROW

Retrieving. He brings back empties. Hey, I'll show you.

Sparrow rolls the empty beer bottle on the floor. The dog jumps down, picks it up in his mouth, and brings it back.

SPARROW

Come on, beauty, here. Get up, beauty. He's all dog. You can make money out of him, Frankie. See what he's good at is catching them squirrels in the park and shaking the dirty peanuts out of them, know what I mean? Only thing, he's trained to chase only one kind of squirrel, and they're getting kind of rare in Chicago on account of the climate's changing. You know what I mean? So he's just hanging around waiting for the climate to change back a little. He's got a real fighting heart. He's dizzy, but he's still in there trying.

Nifty Louie goes to the bar entrance, looks significantly at Frankie, and walks off.

FRANKIE "DEALER" MACHINE

Take the dog up to Zosh.

SPARROW

Frankie, can I go with you?

FRANKIE "DEALER" MACHINE

No.

Frankie follows Nifty Louie up into his building across the street.

Inside his apartment, Nifty Louie takes off his shoe and removes some small packets of powder.

"NIFTY LOUIE" FOMOROWSKI

In a minute, dealer.

He wipes the shoe off and carefully puts it in a closet. Nifty Louie opens the door for Frankie, who comes in, takes off his jacket, and starts rolling up his sleeve. Nifty Louie pulls out a syringe, and Frankie wraps a necktie around his arm.

"NIFTY LOUIE" FOMOROWSKI

Five bucks.

FRANKIE "DEALER" MACHINE

Last time it was two.

"NIFTY LOUIE" FOMOROWSKI

That was more than six months ago, before you went away. They keep raising the price on me.

Nifty Louie takes out a needle and prepares the heroin. Frankie pulls out the money and puts it on the bureau.

FRANKIE "DEALER" MACHINE

They keep doing that, I'll have to find something to take its place.

"NIFTY LOUIE" FOMOROWSKI

The monkey is never dead, dealer. The monkey never dies.

Nifty Louie fills a needle with heroin.

"NIFTY LOUIE" FOMOROWSKI:

When you kick him off, he just hides in a corner waiting for his turn.

Nifty Louie shoots up Frankie.

FRANKIE "DEALER" MACHINE

And the monkey will die waiting. He ain't climbing up on my back no more. Never again, and I mean it.

"NIFTY LOUIE" FOMOROWSKI

Sure, sure.

Frankie takes the necktie off from around his arm and lies down. Frankie's eyes grow dim as the drug takes effect.

Now we are back in Frankie's apartment. Zosh is holding the dog and giving him some beer in a cup. Frankie is in the background.

SOPHIA "ZOSH" MACHINE

Look, Frankie, look how he drinks it. Oh, isn't that cute? Oh, he's got a thirst like a barfly.

Frankie hears the phone ring downstairs and goes to the door. He hears the proprietor answer.

PROPRIETOR

(off camera)

Hello?

SOPHIA "ZOSH" MACHINE

You still expecting that connection to call? For your own peace of mind, forget him.

FRANKIE "DEALER" MACHINE

The doc said I could count on Mr. Lane, and the doc doesn't lie.

SOPHIA "ZOSH" MACHINE

Doc. Look at me. A doc told you I'd be up around in no time, and am I?

He sees some money on a shelf and picks it up.

FRANKIE "DEALER" MACHINE

Have you seen my sticks? See my drumsticks anywhere?

SOPHIA "ZOSH" MACHINE

You know what I'm going to get for this little dog? A little raincoat like for when it rains. Plaid maybe, or maybe all yellow. Huh?

Frankie puts down the money and starts to look for his drumsticks.

FRANKIE "DEALER" MACHINE

Where are my drumsticks, Zosh?

He finds them on top of a high bureau.

FRANKIE "DEALER" MACHINE

How'd they get up here?

SOPHIA "ZOSH" MACHINE

(to the dog)

You liked that, didn't you?

FRANKIE "DEALER" MACHINE

Zosh? I never keep 'em way up here.

SOPHIA "ZOSH" MACHINE

(to the dog)

Drank it all up, didn't you?

FRANKIE "DEALER" MACHINE

Zosh!

Zosh wheels her wheelchair over to Frankie.

SOPHIA "ZOSH" MACHINE

I put 'em there. I stood right up, I walked right over, and I put 'em there, all right?

FRANKIE "DEALER" MACHINE

No? No kidding. How did . . .

SOPHIA "ZOSH" MACHINE

Maybe Vi, when she was straightening up for me. I don't know. Stop picking on me.

Frankie goes over to his drum set and sits down with his drumsticks.

SOPHIA "ZOSH" MACHINE

Frankie, you can't keep stoning yourself about that. There must be a million drummers who play better than you do who can't get jobs. Just remember that, you're going to feel better.

FRANKIE "DEALER" MACHINE

Yeah, sure I will.

Frankie sits down at his drum set and drums on the cymbals.

SOPHIA "ZOSH" MACHINE

Can the noise.

Frankie gets up and picks up the money from the shelf.

FRANKIE "DEALER" MACHINE

What's this for, Zosh?

SOPHIA "ZOSH" MACHINE

What? Oh, Vi. She laid out for groceries. We owe her even more. You got any?

FRANKIE "DEALER" MACHINE

No.

SOPHIA "ZOSH" MACHINE

I don't know what we're doing with all our money.

Frankie picks up a deck of cards and shuffles through them, about to do a trick for Zosh.

SOPHIA "ZOSH" MACHINE

Don't you get enough cards by Schwiefka?

FRANKIE "DEALER" MACHINE

I just do it to kill the pastime. That's all.

SOPHIA "ZOSH" MACHINE

What about my pastime?

Frankie picks up the money again.

FRANKIE "DEALER" MACHINE

What did you say this is for?

SOPHIA "ZOSH" MACHINE

Sick here all the time, you don't even talk to me. We got any more beer? I'd like some.

FRANKIE "DEALER" MACHINE

Beer bloats, Zosh, when you can't exercise.

He fans the deck out in front of her.

FRANKIE "DEALER" MACHINE

Here, pick a card.

SOPHIA "ZOSH" MACHINE

Everything's no good for me. I'm only 25, and it's like I'm a old lady already. Is it my fault I can't exercise?

FRANKIE "DEALER" MACHINE

You want to pick a card, or don't you want to pick a card?

SOPHIA "ZOSH" MACHINE

No, I don't want to pick a card. All I want is just a little . . .

FRANKIE "DEALER" MACHINE

A little what?

SOPHIA "ZOSH" MACHINE

Oh, just a little . . . a little beer, a little fun, a little anything. I can't dance no more. I can't swim, I can't even drink beer. I don't even know what kinds they got here. What other kinds they got these days, Frankie? All right, pretend like I ain't here. It's what you are all the time wishing anyway, like I was killed that night.

FRANKIE "DEALER" MACHINE

I don't wish any such thing. If I don't talk, you get mad; if I say anything, you bite my head off. I don't know whether I'm coming or going anymore, Zosh.

He practices on his drums.

SOPHIA "ZOSH" MACHINE

I told you it gives me headaches.

FRANKIE "DEALER" MACHINE

Well, I gotta practice sometimes, Zosh. When the job comes along, I want to be ready.

SOPHIA "ZOSH" MACHINE

The job, the job. Take them down to your girlfriend, if you gotta practice.

Frankie gets up and goes to her.

FRANKIE "DEALER" MACHINE

What?

SOPHIA "ZOSH" MACHINE

Take them down and give her the headache.

FRANKIE "DEALER" MACHINE

Do you know what you're saying, Zosh? You know what you're talking about?

SOPHIA "ZOSH" MACHINE

Don't give me that innocent look.

FRANKIE "DEALER" MACHINE

I ain't said two words to her since I come back.

SOPHIA "ZOSH" MACHINE

Because I sit here, you think I don't know what goes on.

FRANKIE "DEALER" MACHINE

Not two words.

SOPHIA "ZOSH" MACHINE

I know plenty.

FRANKIE "DEALER" MACHINE

Cut it out, will you, Zosh? Cut it out.

SOPHIA "ZOSH" MACHINE

Take them down to that tramp if you want to make noise. Go on, take them down to her. Why don't you?

FRANKIE "DEALER" MACHINE

All right, I will.

He opens the door and makes to leave. Then he comes back and takes the money.

SOPHIA "ZOSH" MACHINE

Frankie, Frankie, I didn't mean . . .

We are now back in Yantek's bar. A TV is showing a baseball game.

TELEVISION ANNOUNCER

It's a long drive to right field. It's going, going, it's gone. It's a home run.

Sparrow and Vi are sitting at the bar, drinking beer. A blind man comes up to them. We see Molly sitting at a table in the background.

BLIND MAN

I have 12 cents to a beer. If I had 15, I'd be all right.

SPARROW

I've got 6 cents here.

Sparrow and Vi put some coins into his cap.

BLIND MAN

Thanks.

VI

I ain't going to stand for it much longer. The heartaches my old man gives me. You know what he likes to do most? Tear the dates off the calendar. Watching him, that's supposed to be my big Saturday night pleasure. Sometimes he loses all control. Tears off a whole week at once, bleating like a belly goat.

SPARROW

You know what would fill up that empty spot in your life?

VI

Yeah?

SPARROW

A dog.

Frankie comes into the bar and passes behind them.

SPARROW

Ask a satisfied customer. Frankie, that dog I got you makes a big difference in your life, don't it?

FRANKIE "DEALER" MACHINE

Yeah, big.

Frankie goes up to Nifty Louie, who is sitting at the other end of the bar.

FRANKIE "DEALER" MACHINE

I want to see you. I want to see you.

"NIFTY LOUIE" FOMOROWSKI

After the inning.

Zero Schwiefka is sitting at the bar, to Louie's left. He is looking at the TV screen.

ZERO SCHWIEFKA

I'll still bet you six to five.

TELEVISION ANNOUNCER

There's the pitch, and it's a strike. Strike one. London's getting set again, there's the pitch. London swings, and it's a high foul. Roberts trying to get it. It may go into the stands. He's going to try. It's going to be close. Roberts makes a tremendous leap. And he's got it.

Frankie goes over to a table in front of Molly, whom he does not even notice. He stares ahead of him, at Nifty Louie. Molly comes up to him from behind.

MOLLY NOVOTNY

How are you, Frankie? You make out all right with the fellow with the job?

FRANKIE "DEALER" MACHINE

Oh, the drumming job? Yeah, fine, fine. Well, not so fine. He sort of tapped out on me. He promised to call me, but . . .

MOLLY NOVOTNY

It's too bad.

FRANKIE "DEALER" MACHINE

There are a million drummers in the world. How do I rate?

MOLLY NOVOTNY

Maybe he lost your number. It happens. Maybe he's just wishing that you'd keep in touch.

FRANKIE "DEALER" MACHINE

He'd think I was a pest.

MOLLY NOVOTNY

Sure. A good drummer, that's something that don't turn up every day. Go on, Frankie, call him. Come on, Frankie.

Frankie thinks, pulls out a piece of paper, and goes over to the phone. Drunkie John comes over to Molly and pours himself some beer out of a bottle on the table.

DRUNKIE JOHN

Come on, Molly, watch the game, huh?

MOLLY NOVOTNY

I don't feel like it, Johnny. Why don't you go ahead? I'll wait for you.

Drunkie John goes off.

Frankie takes a piece of paper out of his jacket and goes over to the pay phone in the bar.

FRANKIE "DEALER" MACHINE

Yeah, studio B, Monday morning. Fine. Thank you, Mr. Lane. Bye.

Frankie goes over to Molly.

FRANKIE "DEALER" MACHINE

Monday, I got an audition for Monday. Me! Yeah. He told me to join the union, and be ready to work.

MOLLY NOVOTNY

Oh, that's swell, Frankie.

FRANKIE "DEALER" MACHINE

Well, thank you. You know, he did lose my phone number. He'd been trying to find me all week long. Here I was, ready to forget the whole thing. Gee, if you hadn't opened your mouth, I wouldn't have called him.

MOLLY NOVOTNY

Sure you would.

FRANKIE "DEALER" MACHINE

I've got an audition with a big band. Me on TV!

MOLLY NOVOTNY

You practice a lot, right?

FRANKIE "DEALER" MACHINE

Practice. I'll beat those heads to a shred. Only I gotta find a place where. Zosh can't stand the noise. Molly, you suppose maybe I could put the drums in your place and sort of drop in once in a while?

Molly shakes her head.

FRANKIE

Why not? Molly, why not?

MOLLY NOVOTNY

Oh, Johnny wouldn't understand.

FRANKIE "DEALER" MACHINE

So what could he do?

MOLLY NOVOTNY

It isn't a question of what he could do, Frankie. It's like Johnny can't do much about anything. It's a question of what it does to him. I'm all he has in the world. I don't want to hurt him.

FRANKIE "DEALER" MACHINE

Molly, for crying out loud.

MOLLY NOVOTNY

Oh, you don't know, Frankie. A fella like him, sometimes when we're alone . . .

FRANKIE "DEALER" MACHINE

What does he do? Cry? He's a lush, Molly. He's a hundred percent habitual drunk.

MOLLY NOVOTNY

Look, everybody's habitual something. With him, it's liquor.

FRANKIE "DEALER" MACHINE

Please, Molly. Molly-O.

MOLLY NOVOTNY

It isn't just that, Frankie. I don't want us to start with each other again. Look, what you said about us not being good, it was the truth. Even before you went away, I tried to, it just doesn't add up. It never did, it never can.

FRANKIE "DEALER" MACHINE

Well, give it a chance. I told you it would one day.

MOLLY NOVOTNY

All my life has been one day. On and on and on.

FRANKIE "DEALER" MACHINE

I got drums. I'm headed for a good job. Is that so on
and on and on? I make some money, make Zosh well.
What's so on, and on about that? Don't shut me out,
Molly. I'm trying.

"Nifty Louie" Fomorowski comes over to Frankie and Molly.

"NIFTY LOUIE" FOMOROWSKI

You want to see me?

FRANKIE "DEALER" MACHINE

No.

"NIFTY LOUIE" FOMOROWSKI

What do you mean, no?

Frankie goes over to Vi at the bar and hands her some money.

FRANKIE "DEALER" MACHINE

Vi, here. What we owe.

Nifty Louie follows and watches him, glaring.

SPARROW

Frankie, Vi says, can she trust me? Tell her, tell her,
Frankie, what an honest hustler I am.

Frankie goes off past Molly at her table.

MOLLY NOVOTNY

Frankie, I guess maybe you could drop in once in a while.

FRANKIE "DEALER" MACHINE

Thanks, Molly-O.

Outside the Safari Club, men and women in formal dress are coming out. Molly is among them. The waiter comes out behind.

WAITER

See you tonight.

Molly goes back to her building down the street and goes up the stoop. She hears jazz music coming out of her apartment, with Frankie's accompaniment on drums.

She goes into her apartment and sees Frankie playing.

FRANKIE "DEALER" MACHINE

How's that?

MOLLY NOVOTNY

Real nice.

Molly draws down the shade and takes off her shoes. She takes a dressing gown and goes behind a screen to change.

FRANKIE "DEALER" MACHINE

Should have heard what I did with "Perdido" a little while ago.

MOLLY NOVOTNY

Good, huh? I hope the neighbors liked it too.

FRANKIE "DEALER" MACHINE

I'm very big with the neighbors. They keep banging on
the pipes to let me know how much they appreciate it.
I won't let it go to my head, though.

MOLLY NOVOTNY

Okay. Keep playing drums at 5:00 a.m., you'll see what
goes to your head.

**Frankie stops drumming and turns off the radio, which he has
been accompanying.**

FRANKIE "DEALER" MACHINE

You slip me a smile, and I give you my autograph. You
won't have to fight your way through the bobbysoxers
to get to me.

MOLLY NOVOTNY

I bet those bobbysoxers go for you at that.

FRANKIE "DEALER" MACHINE

Ah.

MOLLY NOVOTNY

You tired?

She comes over to him. He gives her a glass of milk.

FRANKIE "DEALER" MACHINE

But in a very nice way. I've been feeling good all night.
I joined the musicians' union today.

MOLLY NOVOTNY

Schwiefka loan you the money?

FRANKIE "DEALER" MACHINE

Him?

MOLLY NOVOTNY

Who did?

FRANKIE "DEALER" MACHINE

Nobody. I'm going to hock the drums.

He takes out a sandwich and offers her some. She does not take it. He eats from it bit by bit.

MOLLY NOVOTNY

Oh, Frankie, no.

FRANKIE "DEALER" MACHINE

I got it figured out pretty good. When I get a job, I'll take an advance and get the drums out again. Meantime, I'll use a practice pad.

MOLLY NOVOTNY

You should have asked Schwiefka.

FRANKIE "DEALER" MACHINE

I haven't even seen him.

MOLLY NOVOTNY

You didn't go to work?

FRANKIE "DEALER" MACHINE

I've been practicing here all night. I quit the game, Molly.

MOLLY NOVOTNY

It wouldn't hurt you to wait a couple of days, Frank.

FRANKIE "DEALER" MACHINE

I wanted to quit. I'm quitting a couple of things.

Molly strokes Frankie's chin. He kisses her hand.

MOLLY NOVOTNY

Is it bad?

FRANKIE "DEALER" MACHINE

Not too bad.

MOLLY NOVOTNY

You shouldn't have started again.

FRANKIE "DEALER" MACHINE

Who knows why I started in the first place. I guess in the beginning, you do it only for kicks. Louie gave me my first shot for nothing. I thought I could take it or leave it alone. So I took it and I took it again and again. One day Louie wasn't around. I nearly went crazy until I found him. Oh, I was sick. I was so sick. You can't be that sick and live. That's when I knew I was hooked. There was a 40-pound monkey on my back. The only way to get along with a load like that is to keep leaning on a fix.

Molly starts to cry. Frankie comes over, strokes her cheek, and wipes her tears away.

FRANKIE "DEALER" MACHINE

Don't. I'm one of the lucky ones, Molly. I kicked it and I'm not too far hooked to kick it again. I've had my last fix. I mean it, Molly. Tell me something, you think those bobbysoxers will really go for me?

MOLLY NOVOTNY

(choking a sob)

You can be such a ham.

FRANKIE "DEALER" MACHINE

Maybe I'll get Sparrow a job with the orchestra. When I can put enough money together, I can get Zosh into a really good hospital so she can walk and dance again. And then maybe . . .

Molly has gone to sleep. He goes over to her, takes her glass of milk, puts it on the counter, puts her to bed, and covers her with a couple of wraps. He shuts off the light, sits in an armchair, and covers himself with his jacket.

Back in Frankie's apartment, Zosh is standing at the kitchen sink, making some coffee. There is a knock on the door.

SOPHIA "ZOSH" MACHINE

Who is it?

ZERO SCHWIEFKA

(off camera)

Schwiefka. Open up.

SOPHIA "ZOSH" MACHINE

Just a minute.

Zosh pushes the dog off the wheelchair, sits down in it, and wheels herself over to the door. Schwiefka barges in, along with Nifty Louie.

ZERO SCHWIEFKA

All right. All right. Where is he?

"NIFTY LOUIE" FOMOROWSKI

Good morning, Ms. Machine.

ZERO SCHWIEFKA

Frankie. Frankie. Where is he?

SOPHIA "ZOSH" MACHINE

What is it? What did he do?

ZERO SCHWIEFKA

What did he do? You know what he did! He quit. No notice, no nothing. He sends word by that mistress that he's through. I had to take the slot myself. Where is he?

He makes to hit her but pulls back. Zosh cringes.

SOPHIA "ZOSH" MACHINE

He wasn't at the game?

ZERO SCHWIEFKA

Would we have been looking for him all over if he was at the game? He eats my bread, six years he eats my bread. He gets put away, I send you money regular. He gets out, I give his job back . . .

"NIFTY LOUIE" FOMOROWSKI

Shut up.

ZERO SCHWIEFKA

What do you mean . . .

"NIFTY LOUIE" FOMOROWSKI

Shut up. You think it was easy talking fellas like Williams and Markette up to a two-bit game like yours?

ZERO SCHWIEFKA

Louie, Louie.

"NIFTY LOUIE" FOMOROWSKI

I sold them on Frankie.

ZERO SCHWIEFKA

Why are we getting excited?

"NIFTY LOUIE" FOMOROWSKI

They fatten the pocket and they're hungry for action. We finally get a chance to score big—and you lose the deal.

ZERO SCHWIEFKA

Look, Louie, I swear. I swear. When Markette and Williams come, the dealer will be there, or a player just as good.

"NIFTY LOUIE" FOMOROWSKI

There ain't none as good. Why didn't you offer him more money, or a piece of the play?

ZERO SCHWIEFKA

From your end of mine?

"NIFTY LOUIE" FOMOROWSKI

What's the difference whose end? Do you expect me to stand here and argue about pennies?

Nifty Louie strides toward the door.

"NIFTY LOUIE" FOMOROWSKI:

Your end.

Nifty Louie goes out.

Outside on a city sidewalk, Molly is standing, looking at the sign on the building in front of her: Musicians' Union Building. Frankie comes out.

FRANKIE "DEALER" MACHINE

Look, I'm a musician.

MOLLY NOVOTNY

Well, how does it feel?

FRANKIE "DEALER" MACHINE

Well, it feels like you better hang on my arm, or I go up like a balloon. I'm a musician.

MOLLY NOVOTNY

Where are we going?

FRANKIE "DEALER" MACHINE

I don't know, but I want to buy you something.

MOLLY NOVOTNY

Ah, no.

FRANKIE "DEALER" MACHINE

I have to spend some money or I'll bust.

They are walking in front of a dealer's showroom. Frankie points out a luxury car.

FRANKIE "DEALER" MACHINE

How about one of those in green?

MOLLY NOVOTNY

Frankie!

They pass in front of a TV store and see one in the window.

FRANKIE "DEALER" MACHINE

Maybe a color TV set; they're pretty.

MOLLY NOVOTNY

Go on.

They move on to another shop window and see an elaborate 1950s kitchen. Two dummies of a husband and wife are also displayed.

FRANKIE "DEALER" MACHINE

Would you look at this production, and only for cooking? Now, who would want a thing like that? Boy, it's goofy, huh?

MOLLY NOVOTNY

It's pretty, huh?

(she points to the male dummy, who is sitting
in a chair in a suit, reading a paper)

I wonder what he does for a living.

FRANKIE "DEALER" MACHINE

Him?

MOLLY NOVOTNY

Must make a nice dollar. Look at the way he dresses, a kitchen like that.

FRANKIE "DEALER" MACHINE

I notice he doesn't help her none, though. I bet he never even married the girl. Look at that, she isn't even wearing a ring on her finger.

MOLLY NOVOTNY

She takes it off when she cooks, maybe, and he's tired after hard day's work.

FRANKIE "DEALER" MACHINE

All right, so let him sit there. But at least he could talk to her once in a while. Doesn't have to sit there with his nose buried in the magazine. I would talk to her.

MOLLY NOVOTNY

What would you say?

FRANKIE "DEALER" MACHINE

I'd say, how you been? How did it go today? What's for supper?

MOLLY NOVOTNY

Steak's for supper, and everything went fine today.

FRANKIE "DEALER" MACHINE

Steak. Good. Now how about you and me stepping out tonight after we eat?

MOLLY NOVOTNY

Why don't we just stay home and turn on some music?

FRANKIE "DEALER" MACHINE

Yeah. I like that better. We'll just stay home and turn on some music.

Frankie kisses Molly on the cheek.

FRANKIE "DEALER" MACHINE

I wish it was Monday already.

Frankie comes into Frankie and Zosh's apartment. Zosh is in a wheelchair, sipping a cup of coffee.

FRANKIE "DEALER" MACHINE

Hi, Zosh.

SOPHIA "ZOSH" MACHINE

Where you been? Schwiefka was here, and said you quit him. Where you been? Why'd you quit him?

FRANKIE "DEALER" MACHINE

I have a tryout on Monday, and if the bandleader likes the way I play, I'm hired.

SOPHIA "ZOSH" MACHINE

Frankie, go tell Schwiefka that you was fooling; you'll deal. Maybe this bandleader won't like how you play.

FRANKIE "DEALER" MACHINE

Zosh, look, I joined the musician's union.

Frankie hands her his union card.

SOPHIA "ZOSH" MACHINE

Why do you gotta go around changing things? Why can't it be like always? Why you gotta quit dealing, Frankie? How we gonna live with no money coming in?

FRANKIE "DEALER" MACHINE

It'll start coming in Monday.

SOPHIA "ZOSH" MACHINE

But suppose they call this great tryout off. You can't tell me it's a sure thing, can you? Frankie, deal for Schwiefka like always. Forget this "great" job.

FRANKIE "DEALER" MACHINE

I quit dealing, Zosh, I can't take the chance. Don't you understand? If the joint gets raided and I get picked up again, Mr. Lane would be through with me. And then how would I play with a band?

SOPHIA "ZOSH" MACHINE

How you're going to play if Schwiefka gets your arms broke?

FRANKIE "DEALER" MACHINE

Go on.

SOPHIA "ZOSH" MACHINE

Yeah, right here he said it, and he wanted to slap me around too. Why can't it be like always?

Zosh starts to tear up the union card. Frankie grabs it from her and shakes her as she sobs. Then he lets go and storms out of the apartment. After he has left, Zosh fingers her whistle anxiously.

In Yantek's bar, we see Nifty Louie, who eyes Frankie as he comes in and goes to the bar. Nifty Louie gives a whistle to Schwiefka, who has been sitting at a booth. They both go over to Frankie at the bar.

FRANKIE "DEALER" MACHINE

Yantek.

Yantek pours Frankie a shot of whiskey.

ZERO SCHWIEFKA

You miserable piece of humanity.

FRANKIE "DEALER" MACHINE

I got a right to quit if I want.

ZERO SCHWIEFKA

Markette and Williams are coming tomorrow. Don't you realize the significance?

FRANKIE "DEALER" MACHINE

Leave me alone.

ZERO SCHWIEFKA

I'll leave you alone in the alley with the cats looking.

"NIFTY LOUIE" FOMOROWSKI

That's enough, Schwiefka. He don't want to deal, he don't want to deal.

ZERO SCHWIEFKA

What are you talking about all of a sudden?

"NIFTY LOUIE" FOMOROWSKI

Don't raise your voice to me, you slob. He's not a slave, you can't force him. So what's the use? You had the best of him all these years. Don't be a pig. He just ain't interested, right?

ZERO SCHWIEFKA

All right. All right. Markette and Williams never heard of him. Money, something to blow your nose on. I wash my hands.

Schwiefka storms off and sits at a nearby table. We can see him in the background.

"NIFTY LOUIE" FOMOROWSKI

He's just a pig is all. Still, you can't blame him so much. Letting the big ones get away on account of the best dealer in the business ain't working for you no more. That ain't easy to swallow. You're the best, all right.

FRANKIE "DEALER" MACHINE

You're a squeeze player, Louie.

"NIFTY LOUIE" FOMOROWSKI

Been tried on you before.

FRANKIE "DEALER" MACHINE

I'm new around here.

"NIFTY LOUIE" FOMOROWSKI

Are we really asking so much, dealer? One night.

FRANKIE "DEALER" MACHINE

I'd like to, but . . .

"NIFTY LOUIE" FOMOROWSKI

You help us make a bundle, we'll spread a little of that
old sunshine around. Couldn't you use a couple of
hundred? Maybe 250, huh? 250 pays a lot of doctor
bills.

FRANKIE "DEALER" MACHINE

Tomorrow, huh?

Schwiefka comes back to the bar and is about to grab Frankie's arm.

ZERO SCHWIEFKA

Frankie . . .

"NIFTY LOUIE" FOMOROWSKI

Let him make up his mind.

FRANKIE "DEALER" MACHINE

Okay. But for one night, win or lose, sun up, I case
the deck.

ZERO SCHWIEFKA

Sure. You're the dealer. What a load off! Now I can
sleep. Take care of that arm.

Schwiefka goes off.

"NIFTY LOUIE" FOMOROWSKI

The character, huh? Were you jacking up the price
just now or do you really have this music job?

FRANKIE "DEALER" MACHINE

If they like what they hear.

"NIFTY LOUIE" FOMOROWSKI

Chancy, eh? Nervous? So what are we waiting for?

FRANKIE "DEALER" MACHINE

Don't talk about it. It's tough enough.

"NIFTY LOUIE" FOMOROWSKI

I know, I know. I put down a craving once. No candy, sweets. I used to be eating it all the time. Got examined for the army. They said you gotta sugar in your blood, friend. You gotta give up sweets forever or it's goodbye, Charlie. I had to give up candy.

FRANKIE "DEALER" MACHINE

My gums bleed for you. It's awful.

"NIFTY LOUIE" FOMOROWSKI

It was. That unfinished feeling you got all the time. Well, I don't have to tell you.

FRANKIE "DEALER" MACHINE

So don't.

"NIFTY LOUIE" FOMOROWSKI

I mean you got this one thing on your mind, all the time. Can't stop thinking about it.

FRANKIE "DEALER" MACHINE

You're just a mine of information, aren't you?

"NIFTY LOUIE" FOMOROWSKI

You know what I did? I said to myself, okay, off sweets forever. Well, forever can start tomorrow, but once in my life I'm going to eat all the candy that I can hold. I bought $18.23 worth of candy, lugged it up to my room. All night long, I ate candy. I was sick, I was sweating. But I kept shoving it in. Ever since then, when I feel like candy, I say to myself, well, you can't complain, brother; you once had it, and had it good. You know what I mean? Huh?

Frankie and Louie go off together, Louie holding Frankie's arm, up to and in Louie's building across the street.

The scene shifts to the Safari Bar. Frankie comes in and goes to Molly at her counter.

FRANKIE "DEALER" MACHINE

How is it, Molly-O?

MOLLY NOVOTNY

All right, Frankie, how are you doing?

WAITER

What will you have?

FRANKIE "DEALER" MACHINE

Couple of ryes.

MOLLY NOVOTNY

All day I was expecting you'd be in to practice.

FRANKIE "DEALER" MACHINE

Practice! I'll get down there and knock them dead. It's all in the wrist, and I got the touch, Molly. Look at that. Steady as a rock. It'll do anything I want it to do.

The waiter brings the drinks over. Frankie gives him a dollar.

FRANKIE "DEALER" MACHINE

Keep the change, pal.

WAITER

Thanks.

MOLLY NOVOTNY

You got a cigarette, Frankie?

FRANKIE "DEALER" MACHINE

Yeah.

Frankie gives her a cigarette and tries to light it, but suddenly his eyes go blank and he blinks in a strange way. He waves the match to put it out.

MOLLY NOVOTNY

You're on it again, Frankie. Why? Why?

FRANKIE "DEALER" MACHINE

No. Listen, Molly, listen.

MOLLY NOVOTNY

Why?

Drunkie John comes over and grabs Molly by the arm.

DRUNKIE JOHN

Molly? Molly?

FRANKIE "DEALER" MACHINE

Beat it.

DRUNKIE JOHN

Molly, I only want to take a walk . . .

FRANKIE "DEALER" MACHINE

Molly, listen to me. I can explain it.

DRUNKIE JOHN

Molly, I just want to talk to you.

FRANKIE "DEALER" MACHINE

Will you get out of here?

MOLLY NOVOTNY

Stop it.

FRANKIE "DEALER" MACHINE

Molly.

MOLLY NOVOTNY

Please don't hurt him, will you?

FRANKIE "DEALER" MACHINE

Go away.

Frankie shoves Drunkie John, who falls down on the floor. The manager comes over, irate.

MANAGER

(to Molly)

You'll lose your job. Can't you manage your customers?

Drunkie John stands up.

DRUNKIE JOHN

Molly!

Both Drunkie John and Frankie grab Molly by the arms. She breaks free and rushes out, the strippers onstage in the background dancing.

Molly rushes out of the bar and across the street to her building. Frankie follows her and runs in front of a car, which screeches to a halt and honks.

Molly rushes into her apartment and locks it.

Frankie comes into the building and knocks on her front door.

Molly hurriedly packs some clothes into a suitcase. She puts on a raincoat and picks up the suitcase and her radio.

FRANKIE "DEALER" MACHINE

Molly. Molly, listen to me. Molly, open the door. Molly, will you open the door? Molly? Let me talk to you. Molly. Molly, Open the door.

Molly comes out and storms past Frankie in the hallway. They go out down the stoop.

FRANKIE "DEALER" MACHINE

Molly, where you going? Molly? Tell me where you going? Molly!

Molly, on the sidewalk, calls for a taxi.

MOLLY NOVOTNY

Taxi.

FRANKIE "DEALER" MACHINE

Will you let me explain? You'll know why I did it.

A taxi pulls up, and Molly gets into it. The taxi goes off, leaving Frankie behind.

FRANKIE "DEALER" MACHINE

(calling after the taxi)

Molly, listen. Will you please let me tell you what happened? Where you going, Molly? Tell me where you going? No, Molly, Molly!

The taxi drives off. Frankie is left standing on the sidewalk, looking stunned. Then, in a zombie-like manner, he crosses the street and goes into Nifty Louie's building. In the window, we can see him in Louie's apartment, taking off his jacket and rolling up his sleeves. The shade is pulled down.

In Schwiefka's poker room, we see Schiefka, Sparrow, and Frankie, seated at the poker table.

ZERO SCHWIEFKA

Don't forget to clean out the kaboon.

SPARROW

I already cleaned it. And say please when you talk to me, or I'll buy a kaboon and go into business for myself. How's that, Frankie? Nothing, huh? Well . . .

FRANKIE "DEALER" MACHINE

I'm reminding you, Schwiefka, I get two, two and a half, maybe more.

ZERO SCHWIEFKA

Would I go back on my word?

There is a knock on the door, and Sparrow goes to answer it.

Several gamblers come in, accompanied by Nifty Louie.

"NIFTY LOUIE" FOMOROWSKI

How you feeling, dealer?

BARFLY 1

How are you, Schwiefka?

ZERO SCHWIEFKA

Ah, big night tonight?

Another knock on the door. Sparrow goes to answer it. Outside are two men: Williams and Markette. Williams is burly, Markette short, with a pencil moustache.

SPARROW

Yeah?

WILLIAMS

This the place?

SPARROW

I don't know what place you mean, buddy. This is the endless belt and leather company. You want to buy a endless belt?

Nifty Louie comes to the door and pushes Sparrow aside.

"NIFTY LOUIE" FOMOROWSKI

Come right in. We just started. How have you been?

SAM MARKETTE

How are you?

WILLIAMS

Good.

"NIFTY LOUIE" FOMOROWSKI

(to Sparrow)

I could handle the door better if I was blind.

SPARROW

Boy, you couldn't heat towels for a scared barber.

"NIFTY LOUIE" FOMOROWSKI

You know Schwiefka?

ZERO SCHWIEFKA

Oh sure. Glad to have you.

SAM MARKETTE

Hi.

WILLIAMS

Hi.

SAM MARKETTE

Are you Machine? Man with the golden arm, huh?

Williams holds out a roll of bills.

WILLIAMS

Let's see you try and take this away.

The men sit down at the poker table, and Frankie begins to deal.

FRANKIE "DEALER" MACHINE

Here we go down and dirty.

We see Vi coming up the alley outside the poker room. She goes up the stairs and knocks on the door. Sparrow answers.

SPARROW

No ladies allowed. You know that, Vi.

VI

Is Frankie in there?

SPARROW

What's the matter?

VI

Zosh, I can't get her to sleep. She and Frankie had an argument and she's almost out of her mind. Is he in there?

SPARROW

Well, I can't call him now.

VI

Well, I just want to know if he's here. I've been bouncing around Clark Street like a pool ball.

SPARROW

He's here. He's here. I gotta get back in.

VI

But I'd tell him she's worried, if you get a chance.

SPARROW

Yeah.

Sparrow goes back in and closes the door. Vi goes off.

Back in the poker room:

FRANKIE "DEALER" MACHINE

Three aces, two pairs. Possible straight flush, aces.

WILLIAMS

200.

SAM MARKETTE

I call it 200, and I'll raise it two.

FRANKIE "DEALER" MACHINE

I'll have a look for 400, and the house bumps you 300 more. Up to you. Ace.

WILLIAMS

I don't know. I just don't know.

SAM MARKETTE

You got three aces; show him.

WILLIAMS

He's got a possible straight flush to the queens showing.

SAM MARKETTE

I tell you, he's bluffing.

WILLIAMS

I think he bluffed me out of a couple tonight. You wouldn't be a jerk enough to try it again, would you?

FRANKIE "DEALER" MACHINE

Bet, and find out.

SAM MARKETTE

Oh, bet, bet. I tell you he is a bluff artist.

WILLIAMS

Call.

SAM MARKETTE

I call it, and I raise it 500 more.

WILLIAMS

Sammy.

SAM MARKETTE

I know what I'm doing.

FRANKIE "DEALER" MACHINE

I'll have a look, and the house bumps you 500 more.

WILLIAMS

I told you. I told you he had it.

SAM MARKETTE

Shut up. Will you let me think?

FRANKIE "DEALER" MACHINE

It's up to you.

SAM MARKETTE

What's the rush, I want to know?

FRANKIE "DEALER" MACHINE

Your bet, two pairs.

SAM MARKETTE

I heard you. I heard you. What is this? A force joint or something? A man's got a right to study his hand.

FRANKIE "DEALER" MACHINE

Bet or fold.

Sammy pulls some more money out of his pocket.

WILLIAMS

Use your head, Sammy. I tell you, he's got it. Don't throw good money after bad.

SAM MARKETTE

I know what I'm doing.

Sam Markette is about to put some more money down, but he sees Frankie clearing the bets off the table.

SAM MARKETTE

What'd you have?

FRANKIE "DEALER" MACHINE

You didn't pay to find out.

Sam Markette grabs Frankie's cards and looks at them.

WILLIAMS

Nothing. Two lousy nines. You let him bluff you out of a full house with a lousy two nines.

FRANKIE "DEALER" MACHINE

You do that again at this table and you'll through.

ZERO SCHWIEFKA

Ah, forget it, this once, dealer. He paid plenty for it.

(Laughter)

WILLIAMS

You are good, dealer, maybe too good.

FRANKIE "DEALER" MACHINE

What do you mean by that?

ZERO SCHWIEFKA

Cut the talk. Deal, deal.

"NIFTY LOUIE" FOMOROWSKI

Punk, get some of this smoke out of here.

Sparrow goes over to the window, pulls up the shade, and opens the window. Daylight streams in.

FRANKIE "DEALER" MACHINE

What do you mean, too good?

WILLIAMS

If the shoe fits, brother.

FRANKIE "DEALER" MACHINE

I'm casing the deck, it's daylight.

WILLIAMS

What?

SAM MARKETTE

Tell him to sit down and deal.

ZERO SCHWIEFKA

Well, we always break up around now.

SAM MARKETTE

One more round.

FRANKIE "DEALER" MACHINE

How about my money?

SAM MARKETTE

Put some more back on the slot.

ZERO SCHWIEFKA

Frankie, how about it?

FRANKIE "DEALER" MACHINE

Nope. Just give me what's coming to me.

"NIFTY LOUIE" FOMOROWSKI

One more hour, huh?

ZERO SCHWIEFKA

I'll deal.

SAM MARKETTE

You? We want to play Machine.

ZERO SCHWIEFKA

Oh, you think I can't show you a thing or two, huh?
Sit down, we'll get going.

FRANKIE "DEALER" MACHINE

How about my dough?

"NIFTY LOUIE" FOMOROWSKI

As soon as we break.

FRANKIE "DEALER" MACHINE

Now.

"NIFTY LOUIE" FOMOROWSKI

Give us a chance to count it at least. Go home. You'll get it later.

ZERO SCHWIEFKA

Okay. Ante up, here we go. A hundred it is.

WILLIAMS

Yeah, a hundred. Okay, here we go.

Frankie comes out of the building, tired and groggy. We see him go down the alley, then follow him as he goes up the stoop of his own building. Vi, wearing a hat, gloves, and a purse, comes down the stoop at the same time.

VI

Good morning, Frankie.

We follow her as she goes down the street.

Frankie, tired and unshaven, goes into his apartment. He takes off his jacket. We see Zosh asleep on the bed. Frankie stretches. Zosh does not move. Frankie yawns, taking off his shoes. Then he gets up, puts his jacket back on, and leaves the apartment. We see him go down the stairs, outside, and down the stoop. He runs back to the poker room. Sparrow lets him in.

SPARROW

Frankie.

FRANKIE "DEALER" MACHINE

Louie is still here?

SPARROW

He's having an apoplexy, but they're doing a sweep in there.

Nifty Louie comes out.

"NIFTY LOUIE" FOMOROWSKI

We're getting murdered. You'll have to take the slot.

FRANKIE "DEALER" MACHINE

I am not here for dealing.

Frankie shows his shaking hands to Louie.

FRANKIE "DEALER" MACHINE

Look, Louie, you have to make it stop.

"NIFTY LOUIE" FOMOROWSKI

No deal, no fix.

FRANKIE "DEALER" MACHINE

Well, give me my money and I'll go see somebody else.

"NIFTY LOUIE" FOMOROWSKI

I can't give you any money now. The house needs every cent.

FRANKIE "DEALER" MACHINE

You owe it to me.

"NIFTY LOUIE" FOMOROWSKI

Take me to court.

FRANKIE "DEALER" MACHINE

Please, Louie, you gotta make it stop.

"NIFTY LOUIE" FOMOROWSKI

I'll take care of you. Just work a few hours.

FRANKIE "DEALER" MACHINE

I have to get some sleep. I gotta be fresh tomorrow.

"NIFTY LOUIE" FOMOROWSKI

You work a few hours. Do us a favor. I'll guarantee you'll feel like a week in the country.

FRANKIE "DEALER" MACHINE

Please, Louie, please, now.

"NIFTY LOUIE" FOMOROWSKI

Drop dead.

FRANKIE "DEALER" MACHINE

Wait a second. Okay.

They go in.

The scene switches to Yantek's bar. Sparrow comes in and goes to the blind man sitting at the bar, drinking a beer.

SPARROW

Louie says you got money for him. Give me. He's waiting.

BLIND MAN

Sparrow?

SPARROW

Yeah, yeah.

BLIND MAN

Yeah, I know he's waiting. So I've seen this one and that one. And they all say the same thing. Tell Louie like he tells us nothing for nothing.

SPARROW

Not a penny?

BLIND MAN

No.

DRUNKIE JOHN

Hey, how is it up there?

SPARROW

What a game. Schwiefka's melting away like a dirty candle.

DRUNKIE JOHN

The dealer's losing, huh? What's happened to that golden arm?

SPARROW

Don't worry about the dealer. The game's just going on a day and a half. He'll come through.

DRUNKIE JOHN

Why not? With those educated fingers. Now you see it,
now you don't.

SPARROW

You keep your dirty mouth off the dealer. Frankie
runs a clean game. There ain't nothing in the world
that would make him change that. Arggh!

Sparrow storms off.

DRUNKIE JOHN

Hey, Yantek?

Back in the poker room, the game is going. Schwiefka is on
the phone.

FRANKIE "DEALER" MACHINE

Piece of hearts, eight of spades.

ZERO SCHWIEFKA

All right. All right.

FRANKIE "DEALER" MACHINE

Six of hearts.

ZERO SCHWIEFKA

Can you let me have a thousand? How about 500?
I know it's Sunday night. I didn't call you up to find
what day it is.

FRANKIE "DEALER" MACHINE

House checks to you?

WILLIAMS

Hold it a minute.

FRANKIE "DEALER" MACHINE

Yeah. Hold it.

Williams goes over to the side and pours some water from a pitcher over his head.

SAM MARKETTE

Give me some of that.

Williams pours some water on Markette's head.

FRANKIE "DEALER" MACHINE

I gotta get out of here, Louie. I'm dead. I ain't slept in almost two days.

"NIFTY LOUIE" FOMOROWSKI

Just a little while now.

FRANKIE "DEALER" MACHINE

It ain't doing any good, the house is still losing.

"NIFTY LOUIE" FOMOROWSKI

Stay with it, dealer. The class is beginning to tell. Just stay with it.

FRANKIE "DEALER" MACHINE

I just can't. My head won't work no more.

ZERO SCHWIEFKA

Louie, Louie, I'm running out of guys to call.

"NIFTY LOUIE" FOMOROWSKI

Lippy.

ZERO SCHWIEFKA

I can't find him.

"NIFTY LOUIE" FOMOROWSKI

I'll find him. He's loaded.

FRANKIE "DEALER" MACHINE

I'm getting out of here.

"NIFTY LOUIE" FOMOROWSKI

Just a little longer while I make a call and I'll take you over to my place.

Williams and Markette go back to the table. The game resumes.

WILLIAMS

Ah, where were we? You patch.

FRANKIE "DEALER" MACHINE

I'll check you.

WILLIAMS

Okay, I bet one hundred.

In the alley outside the building with the poker game, we see Sparrow approaching holding two full paper bags. He climbs up the stairs and is let into the poker room.

MALE SPEAKER

Coffee?

SPARROW

Good and black.

Cheers from the gamblers. A knock on the door. Sparrow lets in Nifty Louie, who approaches Schwiefka.

"NIFTY LOUIE" FOMOROWSKI

I can't raise another cent. How's it going?

ZERO SCHWIEFKA

They're slugging us with their money, every pot almost. They're raising and raising until we're forced out.

FRANKIE "DEALER" MACHINE

What day is it?

"NIFTY LOUIE" FOMOROWSKI

Can't you think of anybody we can tap for a few thousand?

FRANKIE "DEALER" MACHINE

What day is it? Is it Monday yet?

"NIFTY LOUIE" FOMOROWSKI

Listen to me. You listen to me.

FRANKIE "DEALER" MACHINE

Why? Why?

"NIFTY LOUIE" FOMOROWSKI

Listen to me, I said. The next big pot they try to force out with their raising, you gotta stay with them.

FRANKIE "DEALER" MACHINE

Schwiefka don't let me. He keeps nudging me to fold.

"NIFTY LOUIE" FOMOROWSKI

That's because he ain't sure you'll win.

FRANKIE "DEALER" MACHINE

You can't be sure.

"NIFTY LOUIE" FOMOROWSKI

There's a way you can be sure, all right. You can do anything you want with those cards.

FRANKIE "DEALER" MACHINE

That's only for fun. I haven't got enough to do it for real.

"NIFTY LOUIE" FOMOROWSKI

You want to get out of here, don't you?

FRANKIE "DEALER" MACHINE

What?

"NIFTY LOUIE" FOMOROWSKI

You want to get to that tryout in good condition, don't you?

FRANKIE "DEALER" MACHINE

Yeah. I want to get that feeling good.

"NIFTY LOUIE" FOMOROWSKI

Well, then, make sure. You know what I mean.

WILLIAMS

Let's get on with the game. Let's get on with the game.
I feel hot.

The gamblers sit down at the table. Frankie sits down and
starts to deal, looking dazed.

MARKETTE

I'm in.

WILLIAMS

I'm in.

FRANKIE "DEALER" MACHINE
(laying out cards)
Three, King, Jack.

SAM MARKETTE

King bets.

WILLIAMS

Call.

FRANKIE "DEALER" MACHINE

A pair of trays, King, 10, Jack, 7. A pair of trays.

WILLIAMS

I'll bet 200.

SAM MARKETTE

I call the 2.

FRANKIE "DEALER" MACHINE

House bets two, coming out. Pair of trays, pair of
Kings, pair of Jacks.

SAM MARKETTE

I'm back with 500.

FRANKIE "DEALER" MACHINE

(yawns)

House sees.

WILLIAMS

Call.

FRANKIE "DEALER" MACHINE

Coming up. Three trays. Kings, Jacks. Three trays,

WILLIAMS

Three little trays bet 500 bucks.

We see Frankie doing something tricky when shuffling the
cards. Williams grabs him by the wrists, exposing two cards.
He pulls Frankie up and slaps him. Sparrow tries to interfere.
Sam Markette grabs Sparrow and tries to pull off his glasses.

SAM MARKETTE

Take off your glasses. Take them off.

Sam Markette takes Sparrow's glasses off and slaps him
around while Williams slaps Frankie.

ZERO SCHWIEFKA

I didn't know! I didn't know!

WILLIAMS

I'll get to you in a second.

ZERO SCHWIEFKA

I didn't know! This never happened to me before. Eleven years I've been running this game. Ask anybody.

> *(Spits on Frankie)*

You don't deal for me no more.

> *(to Sam Markette)*

You want him?

SAM MARKETTE

I wouldn't dirty my hands.

ZERO SCHWIEFKA

How was I to know? You fellas know that I've been running an honest game. Tell them, tell them.

The gamblers collect their money and storm out of the room. Sparrow puts his glasses back on and walks over on his knees to Frankie. Sparrow pulls him up off the floor.

SPARROW

Frankie. Everything's all right now, Frankie. Hey, Frankie, what's a little cuffing around, huh? Nothing. Am I right? You'll see. And now we'll be in Yantek's, just laughing about it. You should have seen Schwiefka's face when Williams said he'd get to him in a minute. He went white. It was so funny!

FRANKIE "DEALER" MACHINE

Cut it out, you hear?

SPARROW

You was the best sport I knew my whole life.

FRANKIE "DEALER" MACHINE

You hear me?

Sparrow helps Frankie up. Frankie slaps him off.

FRANKIE "DEALER" MACHINE:

Stay away from me, punk.

Frankie knocks Sparrow down, kicks over a chair, and stumbles out of the room.

Back in Nifty Louie's apartment, a tired Louie opens his vest and draws down the shade. A knock on the door. Louie opens the door. It is Frankie.

FRANKIE "DEALER" MACHINE

Hurry, quick!

"NIFTY LOUIE" FOMOROWSKI

Oh, I wanna get to sleep.

FRANKIE "DEALER" MACHINE

Please. Quick.

Frankie barges in.

"NIFTY LOUIE" FOMOROWSKI

Beginning to wear off quick for you, isn't it? You're a graduating student; you're going to have to step it up.

FRANKIE "DEALER" MACHINE

Anything, but please hurry.

"NIFTY LOUIE" FOMOROWSKI

All right. Let's see your money.

FRANKIE "DEALER" MACHINE

Later. Later.

"NIFTY LOUIE" FOMOROWSKI

Right now.

FRANKIE "DEALER" MACHINE

Trust me this once, will you?

"NIFTY LOUIE" FOMOROWSKI

No, I don't do that.

FRANKIE "DEALER" MACHINE

I'll pay you twice as much later. But I gotta do something right now.

"NIFTY LOUIE" FOMOROWSKI

Beat it.

FRANKIE "DEALER" MACHINE

I'll even push for you, Louie. Hurry.

"NIFTY LOUIE" FOMOROWSKI

A flipping junkie always says that.

FRANKIE "DEALER" MACHINE

Please, please, please, Louie.

Frankie grabs at Louie, who fights him off.

"NIFTY LOUIE" FOMOROWSKI

Get your dirty hands off me.

Frankie smashes a chair over Louie's head and back, knocking him out. Frankie starts to rifle the cabinets and closets. But he cannot find anything. Sparrow comes into the room.

SPARROW

Frankie.

Frankie shakes and throttles the unconscious Louie.

FRANKIE "DEALER" MACHINE

(shaking Louie)

Wake up. Get up.

Sparrow tries to get Frankie off Louie.

SPARROW

No.

FRANKIE "DEALER" MACHINE

(to Louie)

Where did you put it?

SPARROW

Frankie, no.

FRANKIE "DEALER" MACHINE

Where did you put it?

SPARROW

Let go, Frankie.

FRANKIE "DEALER" MACHINE

I can't find it. I can't find it.

SPARROW

Let me take you home, Frankie. Frankie, please let me take you home. Frankie. Frankie, please.

Frankie grabs an alarm clock, which reads 9:55.

FRANKIE "DEALER" MACHINE

I gotta be on time. I gotta be on time.

He clips on his bow tie, grabs his jacket, and runs out.

We're now in Shorty Rogers' rehearsal room. The band is playing swing.

Frankie, wearing a suit and tie but unshaven, comes in goes up to a secretary at the door, who brings him up to Shorty Rogers. Shorty Rogers calls the music to a halt.

SHORTY ROGERS

(to the band)

Wow. What's the matter? Come on. Let's try to really cook it.

SECRETARY

Mr. Machine.

FRANKIE "DEALER" MACHINE

Mr. Lane.

SHORTY ROGERS

Okay, can you read music?

FRANKIE "DEALER" MACHINE

Yes.

SHORTY ROGERS

Shelly, let Mr. Machine sit in on this one.

SHELLY MANNE

Number 37. It's right in front of you.

SHORTY ROGERS

You know it, Mr. Machine? Okay, let's try it. 1, 2, 3, 4.

Frankie does nothing.

SHORTY ROGERS

Mr. Machine, the first four bars is all you. Come on, let's try it again. 1, 2, 3, 4.

Frankie drops his drumsticks and picks them up.

FRANKIE "DEALER" MACHINE

I'm sorry.

SHORTY ROGERS

Are you all set? Once again. 1, 2, 3, 4. Okay, Shelly, let's go.

This time, Frankie starts and does well until he starts drumming uncontrollably on the cymbals. Embarrassed and in shock, he walks out.

We now see Frankie going into his building. Louie watches him from the window of his apartment across the street. He has a bandage around his neck from Frankie's throttling. Louie puts on his hat, takes his cane, and goes out.

Frankie rushes into his apartment. Zosh is there.

FRANKIE "DEALER" MACHINE

Zosh, do we have any money? I need some money.

SOPHIA "ZOSH" MACHINE

No. What's the matter?

FRANKIE "DEALER" MACHINE

Some was around here yesterday, wasn't there? I need some money, Zosh.

SOPHIA "ZOSH" MACHINE

Oh, there ain't any. What is it? Frankie? What is it?

Frankie runs out and downstairs. Zosh gets out of her wheelchair to look out the window.

Downstairs at the main entrance, Frankie is about to run out but through the window in the door, he sees Nifty Louie coming up the steps. Frankie rushes into Molly's apartment. Nifty Louie shifts a heavy and menacing ring from the finger of his left hand to the finger of the right and goes upstairs. Frankie goes out of Molly's apartment and out the door.

Nifty Louie walks into Frankie's apartment. Zosh is standing in her bathrobe. Startled, she draws a blanket in front of her.

"NIFTY LOUIE" FOMOROWSKI

You can walk! Since when? What? What's the angle? What are you and Frankie trying to pull? Come on, tell me, one hustler to another, huh? Come on, let me in on it, or I'll croon for it, you hear? I'll tell everybody you can walk. You always could. I'll tell them all, you can walk; you are a phony.

He goes out of the apartment, Zosh following him. They grapple at the head of the stairs.

SOPHIA "ZOSH" MACHINE

No, Louie, Louie, no, you can't do that. You can't tell anybody. Please, Louie.

NIFTY LOUIE" FOMOROWSKI

Let me be.

SOPHIA "ZOSH" MACHINE

Please, Louie.

"NIFTY LOUIE" FOMOROWSKI

Take your hands off.

Louie fights Zosh off, but she pushes him down the stairs. She rushes back into her apartment and sits down in her wheelchair, terrified. We hear:

MALE SPEAKER

(off camera)

Don't touch him. Call the police.

MALE SPEAKER

(off camera)

Did he fall? Was he pushed?

Frankie is walking down a street where construction is going on. He looks at a piece of paper and goes up the stoop of a building.

In front of a hotel door, Frankie knocks on a room where he knows Molly is staying.

FRANKIE "DEALER" MACHINE

Molly, Molly, Molly.

But there is no answer. He sits down in the hallway to wait for her.

Captain Bednar is interrogating Zosh in her apartment.

CAPTAIN BEDNAR

Ain't that the way it happened? They had a fight; next thing anyone knew, Louie was falling. Come on, level, Zosh. Don't try to outthink me. You'll only get tangled.

SOPHIA "ZOSH" MACHINE

I don't know anything about a fight. I was sleeping all morning right here in this chair

CAPTAIN BEDNAR

Then for all you know, it did happen that way. While you were sleeping, Frankie shoved him over.

SOPHIA "ZOSH" MACHINE

He didn't.

CAPTAIN BEDNAR

How do you know, if you were sleeping?

SOPHIA "ZOSH" MACHINE

It wasn't like I was sleeping, it was more like I was dozing, kind of. I'd have heard a fight if there was one. Frankie didn't do it. He wasn't even here.

CAPTAIN BEDNAR

When wasn't he here?

SOPHIA "ZOSH" MACHINE

When it happened.

CAPTAIN BEDNAR

How can you be sure if you was dozing?

SOPHIA "ZOSH" MACHINE

I was up when he left. That's how I'm sure. I saw him go.

CAPTAIN BEDNAR

And he went home this morning?

SOPHIA "ZOSH" MACHINE

But only a second, honest. He didn't get in a fight. He was here only a second.

CAPTAIN BEDNAR

Why didn't he stick around? Was somebody after him?

SOPHIA "ZOSH" MACHINE

Nobody was after him, nobody. He just wanted some money is all.

CAPTAIN BEDNAR

What for?

SOPHIA "ZOSH" MACHINE

I don't know what for.

CAPTAIN BEDNAR

A fix. He wanted it for a fix from Louie.

SOPHIA "ZOSH" MACHINE

It had nothing to do with Louie.

CAPTAIN BEDNAR

How do you know?

SOPHIA "ZOSH" MACHINE

Because there was no money. Why would he want to see Louie for a fix if he didn't have no money?

CAPTAIN BEDNAR

To try and get one without money. Okay. I can wait; wherever he is, sooner or later he is, he's gotta come out for a fix.

Frankie is waiting on the landing in front of Molly's room. Finally she comes up the stairs.

FRANKIE "DEALER" MACHINE

Molly. Molly, wait, please.

MOLLY NOVOTNY

It's finished, Frankie, like I told you.

FRANKIE "DEALER" MACHINE

But I gotta talk to you, Molly, please.

MOLLY NOVOTNY

No, once and for all.

She opens the door and goes into her apartment. She tries to shut him out, but he pushes his way in.

FRANKIE "DEALER" MACHINE

I have to talk to you. Got any money, Molly? I need a few dollars. $10 would do it. I'd get it back to you in a few days or $5 even. Five would be fine. Please. I feel so sick, Molly. I hurt all over. I feel so bad. Don't say no. Please don't say no. Why not, Molly? Why not?

MOLLY NOVOTNY

Jump off a roof if you're going to kill yourself, but don't ask me to help you.

FRANKIE "DEALER" MACHINE

I'll do anything for you, Molly, but right now you have to help me. I need a shot.

MOLLY NOVOTNY

No.

FRANKIE "DEALER" MACHINE

Five would do it, or four, three, or two even. But please hurry.

MOLLY NOVOTNY

You mustn't take that dirty stuff no more.

FRANKIE "DEALER" MACHINE

I know, I know you're right, and I promise, but right now I need a fix, just one fix to help me stop hurting, and then I promise you I'll kick it for good. Just a few hours, Molly. Please.

A knock on the door. Molly opens it partway. It's Drunkie John.

DRUNKIE JOHN

Hello, Molly. I just wanted to come say hello. Ain't you going to let me in?

MOLLY NOVOTNY

I asked you please not to bother me no more.

While Drunkie John and Molly are talking, Frankie is rifling through her purse behind the door.

DRUNKIE JOHN

I miss you.

MOLLY NOVOTNY

Look, I'm awfully tired, Johnny.

DRUNKIE JOHN

I'll stay only a few minutes.

MOLLY NOVOTNY

No.

Drunkie John hears Frankie inside.

DRUNKIE JOHN

Who's in there with you?

MOLLY NOVOTNY

Go away, Johnny, and don't come back.

DRUNKIE JOHN

Who is it? Not the dealer. You ain't hiding him, are you? You wouldn't be dumb enough to be an accessory, would you?

MOLLY NOVOTNY

What do you mean, accessory?

DRUNKIE JOHN

He killed Louie. Cops are looking for him this minute.

MOLLY NOVOTNY

Frankie Machine?

DRUNKIE JOHN

Is he in there?

MOLLY NOVOTNY

No.

DRUNKIE JOHN

I'm coming in.

MOLLY NOVOTNY

Not if you ever want to see me again.

DRUNKIE JOHN

Will you meet me tomorrow?

MOLLY NOVOTNY

Yeah. Yeah. I'll be around Yantek's. Maybe not tomorrow, but soon.

DRUNKIE JOHN

I miss you.

She closes the door on Drunkie John and confronts Frankie.

FRANKIE "DEALER" MACHINE

Honestly, I didn't. What am I going to do?

MOLLY NOVOTNY

Go tell Bednar it wasn't you.

FRANKIE "DEALER" MACHINE

I couldn't. I couldn't stand up to the cops the way I am. Look at me. I'd say anything they want me to say, just for a shot.

MOLLY NOVOTNY

Then get cured first.

FRANKIE "DEALER" MACHINE

What are you talking about? How am I supposed to get cured?

MOLLY NOVOTNY

You did it once.

FRANKIE "DEALER" MACHINE

That was with help and medicine and doctors. I can't go applying to Lexington with a murder hanging over my head.

MOLLY NOVOTNY

Couldn't you do it without going there?

FRANKIE "DEALER" MACHINE

You mean just stop, cold turkey? You don't understand the pain.

MOLLY NOVOTNY

What else can you do?

FRANKIE "DEALER" MACHINE

All I need is one shot, just one.

MOLLY NOVOTNY

All right.

She goes to her purse and takes out money.

MOLLY NOVOTNY

Take it. Go on and take it all, because all that you're going to need after that one shot is another and then another, and then another. Take it. Take it. Why should you hurt, like other people hurt?

Yes, so you had a dog's life with never a break. Why try to face it like most people do? No. Just roll up all your pains into one big hurt and then flatten it with a fix. What do you think you'll find just outside that door? Don't you think that Bednar knows what you are and what you need, just to get through that next hour? Don't you know he's just waiting for you to come and get it? Go on, let him kill you. Let him kill you. It'll be quicker and better than doing it your way.

FRANKIE "DEALER" MACHINE

No, no. I won't let him kill me. No. And I won't run into no grave. But kicking it, a guy can't do it by himself.

MOLLY NOVOTNY

I'll help.

FRANKIE "DEALER" MACHINE

You know what you're letting yourself in for? It ain't pretty. And it could be dangerous.

MOLLY NOVOTNY

If they find you here, then they find you, is all.

FRANKIE "DEALER" MACHINE

I don't mean dangerous from Bednar. I mean dangerous from me. Sometimes a junkie will kill to get away from the treatment, understand? So if you got any knives or scissors in the house, you gotta put them away for a while and don't let me out of the room no matter what I say, or promise, or how much I beg, because if I get out, it'll only be to go out and find a fix. That's the way it is, you understand? Just lock me in the room and if I try to make a break for it, stop me any way you know how, and no matter how much you see it hurting me, don't try to help me with pills or dope or anything else like that. You think you can handle it?

Molly takes out her key and locks the front door. Frankie takes off his jacket and rubs his arm.

FRANKIE "DEALER" MACHINE

Here we go, down and dirty.

Officer Parker drags Sparrow into Bednar's office.

SPARROW

You can't hold me. You are committing double jeopardy or something.

CAPTAIN BEDNAR

Sit down.

SPARROW

You can't hold me. I ain't got all my marbles. You know that, Captain.

CAPTAIN BEDNAR

Write down the cases, Sparrow, and quit horsing around.

SPARROW

I didn't do nothing.

CAPTAIN BEDNAR

But Frankie did something, all right, and I want you to tell me about it.

SPARROW

Whoever killed that peddler should get a ticker tape parade.

CAPTAIN BEDNAR

Yeah, and maybe I'd lead the band. I still want you to tell me about it. Listen to me, Sparrow, when we catch him, he stands trial, whether you talk or whether you don't. The only question is, do I ticket you as an accessory?

SPARROW

Bednar, don't nail me to the cross. He's the only guy I ever had for a friend.

CAPTAIN BEDNAR

He's nobody's friend anymore. He'd mash you with a steamroller if you got between him and a pop in the arm. Come on, talk, Sparrow.

Sparrow stares resolutely ahead of him in silence.

CAPTAIN BEDNAR

Okay, beat it.

Sparrow runs out of Bednar's office.

In Molly's apartment, Frankie is thrashing about madly. He tries to pull open the locked door. He drinks some water from a cup and then from a pot that he fills from the tap. He is doubled over in pain. Then he ties his arm, pulls a sharp black object from a drawer, and tries to inject himself with it, but it is useless. He tears into the bathroom and runs back out clutching a towel. He throws himself down on the bed and thrashes around with severe cramps. He rolls off the bed. He yanks at the door but cannot open it.

FRANKIE "DEALER" MACHINE

Lemme out!

Frankie smashes a chair against the door, but it still does not open, and he collapses with severe tetany.

Now we see Molly coming up the stairs of Frankie's building. She knocks on Frankie's apartment door.

SOPHIA "ZOSH" MACHINE

(inside)

Yes?

Molly goes into the apartment and finds Molly in her wheelchair, pasting clippings into a scrapbook.

MOLLY NOVOTNY

I thought I'd come see how you've been, Zosh.

SOPHIA "ZOSH" MACHINE

Alone, that's how I've been.

Molly hands her a small package.

MOLLY NOVOTNY

Something to eat, sausage.

Zosh grabs the package rudely.

SOPHIA "ZOSH" MACHINE

Alone and worried sick. Where is he? You know where
he is? Did he go to you? What do you want, anyway?

MOLLY NOVOTNY

Zosh, what you told Bednar? You've seen the papers.
You see how bad it makes Frankie look, what you said.

SOPHIA "ZOSH" MACHINE

I didn't tell Bednar nothing. The papers, they twist
everything all up.

MOLLY NOVOTNY

They wouldn't be able to if you didn't let them.

SOPHIA "ZOSH" MACHINE

I can't help what they do. What do you expect me to
do sitting here?

MOLLY NOVOTNY

Just tell Bednar that Frankie wasn't here when it happened. That he didn't do it.

SOPHIA "ZOSH" MACHINE

I never said he did.

MOLLY NOVOTNY

But that's how it sounds, if he was the only one around
at the time, and you know it was somebody else.

SOPHIA "ZOSH" MACHINE

What do you mean? Who?

MOLLY NOVOTNY

I don't know. But maybe Bednar could figure it out if
he didn't think it was Frankie.

SOPHIA "ZOSH" MACHINE

What business is it of yours, anyway?

MOLLY NOVOTNY

I just want to help him.

SOPHIA "ZOSH" MACHINE

Who are you kidding? You think I don't know what
you really want? You think I don't know what you and
him have been up to behind my back while I had to
sit here all these years, had to sit here all these years!

MOLLY NOVOTNY

Oh, Zosh, you got it wrong.

SOPHIA "ZOSH" MACHINE

No, you got it wrong, because you'll never get him. He put me in this chair, and as long as I sit here, he'll never leave me. He knows he belongs to me.

MOLLY NOVOTNY

Zosh, I come only to help.

SOPHIA "ZOSH" MACHINE

I wouldn't want to live if he left me. And I'd rather see him dead too than have him go to you.

MOLLY NOVOTNY

Zosh, please . . .

SOPHIA "ZOSH" MACHINE

Yes, get out of here. Get out of here, you lousy tramp. Get out.

Molly goes out. Zosh throws a newspaper at her. When Molly is gone, Zosh begins to sob.

Back in Molly's apartment, Frankie is walking around, rubbing his arms. He is very cold. He tries to open the door again but fails. He opens the window and is about to jump out when Molly comes in and stops him.

MOLLY NOVOTNY

Frankie, no.

FRANKIE "DEALER" MACHINE

I can't stand it any longer

MOLLY NOVOTNY

Just a little longer.

FRANKIE "DEALER" MACHINE

Please help me. Keep me warm. I can't stand it. I gotta
get out and get a fix. Open the door. Molly, do like I
say, open the door. I'll kill you, I'll kill you.

He lifts a chair and raises it over his head.

MOLLY NOVOTNY

Listen, if you really can't . . .

FRANKIE "DEALER" MACHINE

I can't, I can't.

MOLLY NOVOTNY

Well, then, I do have something put away to make it
stop.

FRANKIE "DEALER" MACHINE

Give me quick. Give me, quick. Where? I'll get it.

She leads him into her closet, rushes out, and locks him in.

FRANKIE "DEALER" MACHINE

Molly, Molly, open the door. Let me out, now, now!
Molly, open the door.

**He keeps beating on the door. Molly puts some loud music on
the radio. Then he stops.**

MOLLY NOVOTNY

Frankie, answer me. Are you all right? Don't think
you can fool me into opening this door, because I'm
not going to. Are you all right? Frankie, please answer
me.

She turns off the music and opens the door. Frankie has been leaning against it and collapses on the floor outside.

FRANKIE "DEALER" MACHINE

Molly, if you love me, kill me, please. Oh, I'm so cold. I'm so cold, so cold. Molly, make me warm, please. Oh, please warm me. Molly, please make me warm. Oh, Molly, I am so cold, make me warm.

Molly covers him with blankets and rubs his hands.

MOLLY NOVOTNY

God. God.

FRANKIE "DEALER" MACHINE

Please make me warm, Molly. I'm so cold. I'm so cold.

Molly lies over him, hugging and kissing him.

The next day, Drunkie John shows up at Molly's apartment and knocks on the door. Inside, Molly is asleep on her bed and Frankie is lying on the floor. He stirs. Molly answers the door partway.

DRUNKIE JOHN

I waited for you at Yantek's last night.

MOLLY NOVOTNY

I told you it might not be right away.

DRUNKIE JOHN

I thought maybe you were sick or something. I just want to tell you don't look for me in Yantek's no more. He threw me out last night. We had a little argument. So make it the Safari, huh?

MOLLY NOVOTNY

Yeah, sure, Johnny, sure.

She closes the door on him.

Frankie gets up, looking weak but better. His hands are no longer shaking.

FRANKIE "DEALER" MACHINE

Pretty good, huh? Molly.

MOLLY NOVOTNY

Take it slow.

FRANKIE "DEALER" MACHINE

Oh, I'm all right. Just a little rocky.

They go to the window and both look out.

Below, on the street, Drunkie John stops to light a cigarette. He sees the two of them looking out the window.

Back in Molly's room:

FRANKIE "DEALER" MACHINE

The most gorgeous day I ever saw. I think it's the first day I ever saw. I got a craving for something sweet. You got anything sweet?

MOLLY NOVOTNY

Sugar.

FRANKIE "DEALER" MACHINE

Give me.

She pours sugar into his hands. He gobbles it up.

FRANKIE "DEALER" MACHINE

More.

MOLLY NOVOTNY

Oh, how can you, Frankie?

FRANKIE "DEALER" MACHINE

Oh, I never felt as good in my life. I feel like all the things inside me have settled into place. Thanks, Molly. Molly-O.

She kisses him.

FRANKIE "DEALER" MACHINE

Oh, God, you'll scrape your face off.

MOLLY NOVOTNY

I don't care.

FRANKIE "DEALER" MACHINE

You got a razor I can use?

MOLLY NOVOTNY

Can I trust you with one?

FRANKIE "DEALER" MACHINE

Cross my heart.

She takes a sack and empties it of kitchenware and other sundries. They see the pile and laugh. He sees a razor and picks it up.

Captain Bednar's car pulls up to Molly's building. Drunkie John and another policeman are riding with him. In the car:

CAPTAIN BEDNAR

Is this the place?

DRUNKIE JOHN

Yeah.

CAPTAIN BEDNAR

Okay, come on.

DRUNKIE JOHN

No, please. You don't need me up there.

The two policemen go into the building. Drunkie John flees.

Inside Molly's apartment, she is polishing a saucepan. She hears a knock on the door. She opens it and Captain Bednar and the policeman barge in.

CAPTAIN BEDNAR

Where is he, Molly?

MOLLY NOVOTNY

He didn't do it, honest.

CAPTAIN BEDNAR

I'm not a judge. They pay me to bring him in. That's all. If you tell me where he is, I promise he'll get every break a junkie can get.

MOLLY NOVOTNY

He's no junkie either. That's finished.

CAPTAIN BEDNAR

Oh sure, you bet.

MOLLY NOVOTNY

You'll see for yourself. He ain't running away from you.

CAPTAIN BEDNAR

So where is he?

MOLLY NOVOTNY

With Zosh.

CAPTAIN BEDNAR

All right, Molly, let's go see.

Frankie goes into his apartment. Zosh is lying in bed.

FRANKIE "DEALER" MACHINE

Hello, Zosh.

SOPHIA "ZOSH" MACHINE

What are you doing here, Frankie? Don't you know Bednar is looking for you?

FRANKIE "DEALER" MACHINE

Don't worry about it, Zosh. I ain't afraid. I didn't do it, you know that.

SOPHIA "ZOSH" MACHINE

Who—who did then, who?

FRANKIE "DEALER" MACHINE

I come to tell you something, Zosh. I'm leaving here.

SOPHIA "ZOSH" MACHINE

But Bednar will arrest you. He told the newspapers you—what?

FRANKIE "DEALER" MACHINE

I'm leaving. You won't have to worry about money or anything. I'll find a way to send you some regular, and Vi will take good care of you.

SOPHIA "ZOSH" MACHINE

Leaving me!

FRANKIE "DEALER" MACHINE

I'm not leaving you, Zosh, just leaving. You saw what happened since I come back. It's like Dr. Lennox told me. I got in the same old routine and before I knew it, I was on it again.

SOPHIA "ZOSH" MACHINE

But you can't leave me. You gotta stay and take care of me.

FRANKIE "DEALER" MACHINE

I know I'm responsible for how you are, Zosh, but I can't go around the rest of my life stoning myself to death about it. I've been carrying my heart ever since it happened. Even now, it hurts me to think about it, but . . . well, it's not that I want to leave, I gotta leave.

SOPHIA "ZOSH" MACHINE

You mustn't leave, Frankie, you mustn't leave.

She clutches at him. He sits down on the bed next to her.

FRANKIE "DEALER" MACHINE

Zosh, say goodbye to me, Zosh.

SOPHIA "ZOSH" MACHINE

You think you're fooling me? I know what's pulling you away. Molly.

FRANKIE "DEALER" MACHINE

No.

SOPHIA "ZOSH" MACHINE

Yeah. You're going just so you can be with that little tramp. Frankie, no.

FRANKIE "DEALER" MACHINE

Goodbye, Zosh.

SOPHIA "ZOSH" MACHINE

No, Frankie, please don't leave! Frankie, no, don't leave.

She rushes out of her bed and is startled to find Frankie with the door open, showing Captain Bednar, Officer Parker, and Molly in the background. Zosh rushes back to her wheelchair pathetically.

CAPTAIN BEDNAR

Get dressed, Zosh.

Zosh gets up slowly and puts on her slippers. She pulls on a bathrobe. She goes toward the front door, but facing Molly, turns and runs out the back door.

Frankie "Dealer" Machine: Zosh, stop!

Zosh rushes out onto the back porch, Frankie and Captain Bednar following. She stops, blows her whistle, flings herself off, and falls to the ground below.

Frankie looks over the railing and sees her body below. He rushes down the stairs, Captain Bednar following. When they reach her, she stirs weakly.

FRANKIE "DEALER" MACHINE

Zosh, stop. Zosh, don't move. Don't try to talk. You're going to be all right.

SOPHIA "ZOSH" MACHINE

Just that I love you so much.

FRANKIE "DEALER" MACHINE

Zosh.

Zosh dies. An ambulance arrives. An attendant rushes up to her, tries her pulse, and listens to her chest with a stethoscope. He places her arms on her chest as is done with the dead. He and another attendant carry her into the ambulance, her face and body covered.

Frankie stands to his feet. Sparrow is there. He and Frankie go off.

On the street, we see Molly coming down from Frankie's building onto the street. Rounding the corner, she sees Frankie and Sparrow and goes up to join them. Frankie and Molly walk together. Sparrow stays behind on the corner. The camera focuses on Molly and Frankie walking side by side. He has a weary but victorious look on his face.

In the background, we see Sparrow shuffle off and Captain Bednar and Officer Parker get into the police car.

THE END